DISCOVERING THE DOCTOR

MASTERSON COUNTY BOOK 2

CALLE J. BROOKES

DISCOVERING THE DOCTOR

LARGE PRINT EDITION

Copyright © 2017 by Calle J. Brookes

For information contact:

www.callejbrookes.com

Book and Cover design by C.J. BROOKES

First Edition: 2017

REED: 06052020

10 9 8 7 6 5 4 3 2 1

1

HER SISTER PHOEBE'S MARRIAGE THAT afternoon had changed everything about Philippa Tyler's world.

Phoebe had been the center of their family since they'd lost their mother almost two and a half years ago. She'd handled the day-to-day running of the Tyler ranch where they had all lived. Kept them all going through some of the darkest days of Pip's lives.

And she'd taken over the raising of Pip's youngest three brothers.

Pete, Parker, and Patton were going to be Pip's responsibility for a while. Until the Tylers figured out what to do next. Phoebe's marriage changed everything. For everyone.

Phoebe and her new husband, the sheriff of their county, hadn't wanted to wait to marry after they'd nearly been killed. No one really blamed them. Pip didn't.

Joel Masterson adored her sister. And had risked his life to keep her sister safe.

Phoebe being married to one of the county's most prominent citizens meant the isolation Pip had always counted on for their family at the Tyler ranch was no more.

Tonight at the wedding reception she'd been forced to deal with far too many people for her sanity. She'd had to escape before she lost the ability to breathe completely.

For Pip, escape had always meant one place.

The horse barn.

Sky Dancer, the gelding she herself had delivered when she'd been only sixteen, whickered when she entered the stable that would be his new home. Pip greeted him quietly then rubbed against the soft nose. This was one of her babies, and she would miss seeing him every day.

She liked horses far better than she did people. There was no doubt about that in her head.

Horses weren't as mean, as malicious, as people. It was as simple as that.

The itch to ride was hard to resist. Pip slipped out of the small jacket that covered her only piece of formal wear, a pale pink dress that was a bit too tight, and far too short. She didn't like dresses much, always feeling exposed and naked in them.

She was more comfortable in flannel and jeans. But for Phoebe, she'd made the effort.

They'd come so close to losing her older sister, just like they'd lost their mother so abruptly.

None of her family took that lightly. If Pip had to step up and fill Phoebe's shoes with the rest of the Tylers, then she would.

She'd just do what she had to do; but tonight... tonight she just needed to get away. To ride. And that was what she did.

DR. MATT MASTERSON, THE ONLY VET IN Masterson County, knew pretty much every horse on the property jointly owned by him and his brothers. And he knew the big bay gelding shooting across the field just as the sun was setting.

He even knew the redhead riding like the wind.

First, the horse was distinctive, and belonged to his brand-new sister-in-law. Second, there were only a handful of redheads quite that small anywhere in Masterson County. Third, there were only four women he'd ever seen ride like that.

One redhead was inside, coordinating the party as his family's housekeeper, the eldest redhead had just been carried away in his brother Joel's arms, and the third had just left to work her shift at the Masterson General Hospital, along with his younger brother Nate.

That left little Pip as the only real possibility.

Pip.

The quiet one. The one who looked at the world with fear. He had yet to figure her out. She was so afraid, especially of men, yet when faced with losing a loved one, she was the bravest woman he had ever seen.

He'd never forget seeing that bravery in action. He still dreamed about that day, about her, in the middle of the night.

Something about the quietest Tyler sister had stayed with him. From the moment he'd dragged her from a raging river and covered her body with his own while a madman tried to kill them all. He'd thought of that woman nightly, at least, ever since.

He stepped up to the fence and just watched as she flew across the field, the animal beneath her. He could almost sense her hurt, her confusion.

Her fear. It was that fear that kept him from acting on the attraction that burned in him—even months after that day.

A luxury sedan slowed on the highway that bordered their pasture, across the field, and Matt suspected he wasn't the only one captivated by the sight of the fairy—every Tyler female looked like a damned fairy—flying across the field on the back of a red unicorn.

She slipped from the back of the horse and began walking him down. Matt made certain to stay in the shadows.

Matt didn't want to frighten her. Pip was so easily frightened.

He had yet to figure out why.

2

Rowland Bowles was a self-taught man, and had made his first five million by his twenty-fifth birthday. He knew a good story—and he knew the people to play in those stories. When given the chance, Rowland preferred to use locals at each location. He loved discovering unknown talents. Of making careers. It gave him a sense of power, and his work a sense of authenticity that many in the film industry tried to emulate.

Very few succeeded. At thirty, he was confident in his skills, and just cocky enough to expect everyone to give him what he wanted. Because he was Rowland Bowles.

Masterson County, Wyoming, was the perfect

place for the script he'd written himself. It was a genre mashup of fantasy and American Western. He had a particular type of world and characters in mind. He had most of the principals already cast, but he'd lost his Gretta and still needed to find his Keith among the local yokels. The actress slated to play Gretta had unfortunately found herself on the wrong end of the law. It hadn't been pretty. And he'd struggled to find the right Keith in Hollywood.

Masterson County shouted authentic Western. How could it not? Everywhere he turned was another cowboy or cowgirl. Beautiful cowgirls, like the trio of redheads he was attempting to follow into the quaint little country diner. They were quite young—early to midtwenties, at most—and very small. The largest was probably just a bit over five four or so, and a whopping one hundred thirty pounds. Maybe. The other two were even smaller, and looked enough alike to be twins. One wore full Western wear and looked like the real deal. Bowles barely looked at her. It was her twin who had caught his attention. The pale pink hospital scrubs were nearly the same shade of pink as the dress worn by the woman he'd seen just two nights before.

The small town—hell, the entire county—was perfect for what he'd wanted. And the night he'd taken the car and driven around the country roads himself had just shown him one thing.

His Gretta. Soft, feminine, sweet. Sexy. The girl he'd watched ride the other night would be perfect for Gretta, sister of the hero. Gretta was soft and wounded, and the hell she'd gone through triggered a rush of powerful magic that damned near destroyed her. Rowland wanted that redhead. He'd get her.

No matter what he had to do. But first he had to deal with Dr. Matt Masterson, his new personal nemesis.

3

MATT WASN'T PLEASED WITH HIS LATEST duties, but the town had banded together and nominated him and his brothers as hosts for the last group Matt ever wanted to see in his town.

The knowledge that Rowland Bowles, the legendary hotshot film director, wanted to use several ranches in Masterson County to film his latest so-called masterpiece had thrilled the locals—and the town board. Tourism wasn't exactly a big money maker in Masterson.

As Mastersons and prominent citizens, he, Nate, Joel, and Levi had been nominated to see that the film crew had everything they wanted and needed. None of the brothers had been too happy about it, but since Matt had been the only one not at the meeting due to a sick-horse call, his loving brothers had pawned the director and his half dozen assistants off on Matt.

He'd be getting back at Joel, Nate, and Levi first chance he got.

Bowles wanted to use the Masterson homestead as one of their sets. Matt was not the least bit thrilled about that.

Worse. Bowles himself had been in that damned sedan, watching Pip the evening of the wedding. And the man wanted her.

Badly.

There was no way that was going to happen. Matt wasn't about to let it. A guy like Rowland Bowles would terrify her.

"What exactly are you going to be needing from the people in this county?" Matt asked as he and Bowles watched the trio of beautiful redheads cross the street. Matt had seen Pip and her two sisters when they'd pulled in. Pip's truck was a distinctive orange and white. He'd watched them for a while as he'd half listened to Bowles chatter on. "We are busy people with busy lives around here. And we like our privacy."

"Of course. I'm very respectful of location

characteristics, Dr. Masterson. Tell me, those women there, do you know them?"

"You might say that. One's my housekeeper. Their oldest sister is currently on her honeymoon with my brother. They'll be back in a few days."

"So you know them. Tell me about them?" Bowles sounded too damned eager, didn't he? Matt fought the instinctive urge to tell the man to just back off.

"They're busy people who really like their privacy." Matt watched Perci turn to her sisters and walk backward a few steps. He heard their laughter from where he and Bowles stood. Light, beautiful, perfect. "Why?"

"That redhead in the pink. I want her. For my Gretta, I mean. Although, she certainly is beautiful, and if she wanted more—well, I'd make an exception to my business-only rules."

"Yes, the twins are gorgeous women."

"Twins?" Bowles puzzlement was clear. "Oh. I didn't realize the other one actually was her twin."

Matt looked at the man like he was an idiot. Even clear across the street, it was hard to miss the fact that Perci and Pip looked exactly alike.

"They're identical. Only difference is a scar. And clothes, of course."

"Is there? Interesting. I don't think it was the other one I saw. Is she actually hiding between the other two?" Bowles winced. "I'm sorry. You said they were family. I don't mean to be insulting. I just know who I need when I see them."

"Pip is just as beautiful as her sister. Brave. Loyal. Talented. Don't discount her simply because she's shy."

"Oh, I'm not, of course. Will you introduce me?"

"Not at the moment. But I do have a two o'clock meeting with Pip Tyler about a horse. You can watch, but I won't lie; you'll intimidate the hell out of her. That'll make me cranky, understand?" He didn't know why he said it, but Bowles put his back up for some reason. Maybe it was the way he was so dismissive of a woman Matt admired more than so many others. Maybe it was the way he was eyeing the Tyler sisters like they existed only to give him what he wanted. To please him. "You can stand back and watch, but that's it. What the hell do you even think you saw out there that night, anyway?"

He had his suspicions. That pricey sedan

Bowles had driven up in had been rather distinctive. And familiar.

"A beautiful red horse, with a small fairy on its back. She wore a thin pale dress, and her hair flew out behind her. It was nearly as red as the setting sun. She flew on that horse. Stunning. She'd be beautiful as my Gretta. I want her. I'm willing to pay her, too. A great deal. Those who star in my movies go on to great things, Dr. Masterson. Great things. I can offer her a way out of this little town if she wants it."

Matt threw his head back and laughed. If Bowles ever figured it out—well, there was no way little Pip would ever give Bowles what he wanted. "Let me know how that works out for you."

4

Rowland studied the cowboy next to him. They were of the same size, though he thought Masterson might have an inch on him or so. Thirty pounds heavier, possibly. Maybe more. Rowland worked to keep himself in shape, but this cowboy was the real deal.

Guy had the kind of good looks women flocked to the theaters to see, he had to admit. If he was filming a romance, this guy would look beautiful next to Gretta. Strong, rugged, dark-haired, blue-eyed. Quiet, but confident.

Dr. Matt Masterson didn't like Rowland's interest in those redheads. That was abundantly clear. Did the guy have one staked out for himself? Rowland understood. What man wanted someone like him coming in and taking away some guy's woman? "I won't touch her, if you have a prior claim, Doctor."

Masterson's countenance darkened. "You won't touch any of them, unless one of those girls asks you to. We're mighty protective of the Tyler sisters around here. They've been through enough recently. All of them. The eldest is my brother's wife. My brother, the sheriff...he takes protecting his wife's family pretty damned seriously."

Rowland had misjudged, hadn't he? Something more was going on with the Mastersons and the Tylers. That had just become perfectly clear. Always a student of people, Rowland wanted to probe deeper, find out more. "I'll watch your appointment with this Pippy, and I'll even behave myself while I do."

"*Pip.*"

"It's not her I want, anyway. It's her sister. And I'll have her, too."

Masterson laughed outright. Like Rowland was an idiot or something. "You go anywhere near Perci Tyler with that attitude, and she'll use a scalpel to teach you some manners. Girl's got teeth—and she's not afraid to use them."

"I'll keep that in mind." Rowland wasn't too worried. A small-town woman would cave in to the idea of what he could offer her. He had no doubt about that. He'd done it time and time again. He'd have Perci Tyler as his Gretta before the week was out.

With or without Matt Masterson's help.

As two more Mastersons—they truly did look perfect as cowboys—hailed his reluctant host, Rowland watched the trio of women enter the diner.

He was hungry.

Rowland just hoped the place had something gluten-free.

He started across the diner.

Masterson called his name. Rowland looked at the other guy. He wasn't about to let some small-town hick keep him from getting to his Gretta. Period.

"Might keep in mind what I said," Masterson warned.

"I'll do that." It didn't mean he had to listen, though.

5

MATT WANTED PIP TO MEET HIM AT HIS VET clinic at two. She had almost two hours until then. Masterson wasn't exactly a big city—the town itself only had about eight hundred people in it—but it was big enough at times to freak Pip out.

Crowds of any kind were too much for her. But she dealt. Silently.

She wasn't about to lose out on this time with Perci and Pandora because she had panic attacks whenever more than three tables in the diner were occupied.

Perci squeezed her elbow. Always there. Just like Pan, the youngest sister, used to be. Until she'd left them to be the Mastersons' housekeeper.

When Phoebe returned from her honeymoon in a few hours, she'd effectively become Pan's boss. No real change there. Phoebe had been bossing from the moment Perci and Pip had been born. Some things would never change.

They took the last booth on the left. Macy, the owner's granddaughter, a woman a year or so older than Pip, nodded when they walked by—she had her hands full. The place was crowded.

With people Pip didn't recognize. She bit back the panic. She was safe.

Her sisters were right there. Two men near the back were first cousins. And there, right in the corner booth on the right was the sheriff of Masterson County and his brand-new bride.

Phoebe was back. And Pip was safe. She'd just have to keep reminding herself that.

She changed direction, aware of Pan and Perci following. They all took turns hugging Phoebe. The eldest sister smiled and told them all about her three-day honeymoon, beaming as she spoke. Joel hadn't been able to take any longer than that, so they'd made the best of the time they had had.

And Phoebe hadn't wanted to leave the boys for too long. They'd had a family meeting—Joel included—right before the wedding to discuss how things at the ranch were going to have to change.

It would take some adjusting for all of them, but Phoebe was moving in with Joel at the Masterson ranch a few miles away. She'd still be around during the day—Joel would drop her off on his way in to town each day. Either her husband or one of his brothers would pick her up each evening after the chores on the family place were done. After the boys' homeschool and Phoebe's drove of Angora goats were tended each day. It wasn't ideal, but it would work.

It meant Pip would have to step up with the boys of the evenings, too. Perci could help on her nights off, but her sister often put in five twelve-hour days at the hospital. On her nights off, she needed to rest. And handle other chores that built up around the place while she was gone.

Perci helped where she could—probably too much.

Change. It was never easy for Pip.

They were halfway through their meal when three tall, gorgeous men approached. Pip's hands immediately slicked with nerves as Matt and Nate moved an empty table up to the edge of their booth.

"Family reunion?" Levi asked, smiling at Pip and Perci as he settled into the chair nearest Pan. "Ok, the scrubs tell me which is which today."

Nate glowered at them both. "Persephone's scar is on the left. Pip's is on the right. Not that hard to remember."

He was right. Perci had a scar just above her left eyebrow from the accident that had killed their mother. Pip had one near her right eyebrow that she'd received when Tom Rutherford had nearly killed her older sister and Joel.

Pip shivered when the men turned to look at her and the scar.

"It's because you dropped him on his head," the brother beside her said. "He's been difficult to teach ever since."

Matt. Matt was the calm quiet one. The one who'd pulled her from the river when she'd swam in to rescue Phoebe that day. The one who'd covered her and her sister with his own body when bullets had been flying around. Matt had been the one to protect.

She trusted Matt. He was the one brother who didn't scare her all the time, the one she could sit next to and not have a panic attack. The one who she liked talking to.

Pip forced herself to relax. Even though she could smell the woodsy scent of his aftershave, could feel the warmth of his big body next to her.

Pip shivered. For a strange moment she wanted to almost snuggle up against that warmth and forget the crowd around her. That was crazy, wasn't it?

She trusted these men. She was safe. She had to learn to stop freaking out every time one of them got close to her, didn't she? Pip concentrated on eating her lunch and following the conversation around her. She'd spent four years pretending not to panic every time something scared her—she'd gotten good at making her family believe she was fine. Today would be no exception.

Fake it until you make it, after all.

Pip looked up at Perci and Phoebe—who shared the bench seat with Joel—a few minutes later. Looked up in time to see her sisters both pale. To hear Perci's low curse and Phoebe's surprised gasp.

Pip turned to look for herself.

6

Matt knew something significant had just occurred, but for the life of him he didn't know what it could be. He looked over his shoulder, following his sister-in-law's gaze.

"Pip, no. Don't look," Perci ordered sharply. "Just get your stuff. Macy will let us out the back way."

Everyone at the table quieted. Levi and Nate shifted closer to the redheads next to them. Matt slipped his arm behind the one closest to him automatically as her sisters looked at her. Whatever had happened, it involved Pip somehow.

Matt studied the trio of men who had just entered. They weren't hard to recognize. Clive Gunderson had lost the election to his own brother for sheriff just the year before. The two younger men next to him looked enough like him to be his sons.

"Phoebe? What's going on?" Joel asked.

"Gundersons," Phoebe said, disgust and—if Matt wasn't mistaken—a trace of fear in her tone. "And they hate us more than the Rutherfords ever did."

Matt could feel the tremors that went through Pip the instant they began. What in the three hells had happened to this woman? And how did it involve the former sheriff and his sons?

Pan wrapped her hand around Pip's. "So... what do we do?"

"You do nothing. You have just as much right as any damned Gunderson to be in this diner," Nate said, glowering at them all. "No one's going to bother you or your sisters here."

"It's not Gunderson that's the problem. It's his son on the left," Perci said, hotly. "That sonofabitch is nothing but trouble."

"Perci, I'm ok. I can certainly be in the same room," Pip said, calmly.

So calmly Matt knew the woman beside him lied. He felt the fear running through her. Felt it.

So why was she lying to her sisters?

And what had the younger Gunderson done to her?

"You shouldn't have to." There was a world of guilt in Pip's twin's tone. Did anyone else catch it? Matt shared a look with his eldest brother. Joel met his eyes and jerked his head toward the door. Matt understood. He'd have to move before Pip could.

But if there was something that significant in the damned diner, he wasn't about to let Joel's sister-in-law face it alone.

Pip was getting a Masterson escort out of the diner. No one would dare mess with her then.

No one did. Pip insisted they all stay and finish their lunch. And outwardly she seemed calm and composed. But Matt knew. It was hard not to. Did anyone else see it? When it was time to leave, he stood first and automatically put a hand on her back. Pulled her closer.

He didn't miss the Gundersons' expressions when they looked at the four redheads walking by them. Or miss the way the younger Gunderson stared—at Pip and her twin.

As if he were trying to place them? Figure out which one was which?

Like Nate, Matt knew he'd never had a problem telling the two apart. They were as different as night and day. But both had a spine of steel and bone-deep loyalty to their family.

They didn't deserve to be afraid any longer.

7

PIP KEPT THE PANIC HIDDEN AS SHE LAID EYES on the man who had attacked her four years ago. He was just a man. Not an overly big one—he was certainly no bigger than her father, who was around five ten and one hundred seventy pounds. But that was still far bigger than she was.

She'd fought him off as best she could, but she knew the truth. If Perci hadn't just known Pip was in trouble and brought herself and Phoebe and Pan to rescue her, he would have succeeded in raping her.

The men walking at her sides—and the four Masterson brothers made darned good walls—were far larger, stronger. If Jay even looked at her funny, she had no doubt Joel would be there to protect her.

The same way Jay's father had protected him all those years ago.

Joel would never terrorize a family of young girls to protect his would-be rapist son.

What the Gundersons had done to her had been wrong.

She shouldn't have to be afraid of them anymore. Pip tilted her chin in the air and walked right by their table. It was time she stopped letting them dictate her life *now*. If she wanted to eat in the diner with her family, she would.

She pulled in a deep breath just as Matt's hand landed on her back and he pulled her closer.

She looked up into kind blue eyes and felt a bit more of her world right itself.

Just as she had from the moment he'd pulled her from a raging river.

8

Jay Gunderson fought to keep his breathing contained, using the control he'd developed over the last four years in prison. He hadn't expected to see his Pip again quite so soon. At least not in reality.

He'd dreamed of the last woman he'd touched every night for four damned years. The dark blue eyes, so soft and vulnerable, staring up at him as he touched her. The red hair that practically burned in the light, but was as soft as silk beneath a man's hands. He'd had his hands in that hair once.

He'd long remembered the sweet taste of her trembling mouth beneath his own.

At first he'd thought the more outgoing twin Perci was closer to his type. But once he'd tasted her sweet, shy, vulnerable twin sister, he'd learned the truth.

Prison had just cemented his hunger for her. It hadn't started right away. Before he'd even been inside six months, she'd just been another bitch he wouldn't mind laying. Or her sister had been, anyway. He'd barely been aware that they had been twins until that last night when he'd seen Perci laughing at him with her sisters.

Four smoking-hot redheads who thought they were too good for a man like him. When Perci had rejected him, he'd wanted to show her entire family what she would have been missing.

Pip had been beautiful, soft where her sister was a ball-busting bitch.

Jay had come on a bit too strong, and he knew it. He hadn't realized how innocent she was. Her blue eyes had haunted him practically ever since.

He watched Pip walk right by him and ignore him. Like she had forgotten who he was. He hadn't forgotten her. He never would.

It took him a moment to figure out which one of those damned Masterson brothers was walking at her side. He'd heard the Tylers were connected to the Mastersons now.

The whole lot of them looked exactly alike and were arrogant pricks. It had been the eldest brother who had arrested him four years ago, on an anonymous tip, of all things.

And then took the position of sheriff away from Jay's father.

Now it was one of Masterson's brothers who was taking her. Who had his filthy hands on her.

Jay bit back the anger that had been his constant companion for years once again.

He would have her again.

It was just a matter of time.

9

They didn't wait until two. Matt kept one hand on her spine as they walked the quarter of a mile from the center of town to his clinic.

The rescue organization had called; they'd wanted to bring him a special horse in need of re-habilitation and resocialization before she could find a permanent home.

He pushed the anger away.

To be honest, he'd wanted to refuse until he'd heard the animal's story. Matt just didn't know when he'd have the time to work with her.

That's where he hoped the woman still shiv-ering next to him came in. He easily sensed the scene in the diner had upset her more than she was telling him. "I need your help."

She looked up at him, her eyes telling him all he needed to know. She hadn't been paying the least bit of attention to where he'd been leading her, had she?

She'd just let him lead her away.

Matt wanted to turn back. Blacken both Jay Gunderson's eyes for whatever it was he'd done to her.

Maybe someday he would. Just on principle alone.

Just to erase that look in her eyes. Matt fought the urge to pull her closer and reassure Pip that everything would be all right. To kiss her and promise to keep her safe from everything for now until eternity. "This way. The rescue I'm affiliated with called me this morning. They're bringing me a quarter horse who's had a rough road. Rumor is she only responds to a few people. And to be honest, I don't have the time to devote to her right now. I was wondering if you can help me move her, if possible. Levi should be done with the far barn on our place in a week or two. I want to stable her there. It's away from Rollo and the rest of our horses. She's not too keen on males in her space at all, I think."

Rather like the woman next to him.

He wanted her help with a horse. That was a simple request. One Pip had no doubt she could meet. Some of the tension filling her lessened. Became more manageable. Of course, it helped that Matt's clinic was on the outskirts of town, far away from that damned diner. She hadn't been there before—they used a vet located just over the county line for their livestock—but she'd heard good things about him.

More, she knew he genuinely loved the animals in his care.

He'd purchased two of her quarter horses just a few months back, after Phoebe had been hurt, when they'd needed money to pay the hospital for Phoebe's care.

She'd planned to wait a year or two longer and get a higher profit, but that hadn't been in the cards.

They were the first of her horses she'd ever

sold. It had broken her heart to watch him drive away with them. But she'd done it. And she knew the two geldings she'd trained as cutting horses would always be well taken care of.

Now that her sisters lived on his property, she'd even see those horses occasionally. Pip had to admit it had worked out well for them.

But that meant she was basically starting back a few paces on her plans to build her own AQH breeding program. She'd been meaning to invest the money from those horses back into her program eventually. Instead it had gone to the Masterson General Hospital. Just like every other spare penny the family had. They were still paying hospital bills from the wreck that had killed her mother and injured both Perci and her brother Phoenix. And bills from the heart attack her father had had after.

The loss of profit from those horses was just another setback.

She was a Tyler. Tylers handled setbacks. It was kind of their stock in trade.

She waited next to the man while the rescue organization's trailer backed in. It was a good rescue. She'd heard of them before. Some of the tension filling her started to relax.

It always did whenever Matt was close by—after the initial panic that a man like him was so close receded.

He made her feel at peace. Relaxed in a way she hadn't been before.

They both knew what they were doing, and she and Matt worked quickly, with the need for only minimal communication between them.

The trailer was backed to the paddock behind the clinic, and everything was ready.

The horse refused to come out. Even with the handler.

Pip knew patience was sometimes the only thing that worked with some animals. Heck, she understood it herself.

Sometimes the world was a very frightening place.

The instant Matt entered the trailer to try to help, the horse protested.

Matt stepped out quickly.

Pip heard the horse inside, heard the fear.

"She's afraid. So very afraid," she said. "You're both big men. Threats. How was she loaded?"

She looked at the man who'd driven the truck from Montana.

"We were set to have two of us, but Charlie's

mom called, and she had to go. Family emergency. Charlie loaded her."

"Let me go in. See if I can calm her some."

10

MATT DIDN'T KNOW A DAMNED THING ABOUT this horse, not really. The thought of Pip getting close to such an unknown didn't sit well with him. But they had to get the horse out. "Step in. See what the situation is. I don't like this, Pip. The risks—"

"Are there for anyone working with an animal this size." Pip looked at him straight on, confidence in her stance once again. The woman lost her fear of the world when it came to horses. Forgot everything but the animals that she loved.

Matt stayed close, ready to pull Pip out of the trailer if necessary. He knew he was probably being a bit too cautious, but something about her made him want to wrap her up and just keep her safe.

Protected.

Was that so wrong?

Maybe it had something to do with the first few times he'd met her after she'd sold him a pair of cutting horses. He'd for damned sure never forget pulling her from the flood. Of holding her close as Rutherford took potshots at them all.

He'd practically had her imprinted on his body for days after that.

Maybe it had been more than that. Maybe the need to protect her had just burst from that day?

She could have died in that river. Most likely would have, if he and his brother Nate hadn't shown up to help.

Her sister most definitely would have drowned. And Rutherford would have shot Perci. Pip could have been shot—or drowned herself. If he and Nate hadn't been there at that exact moment.

Matt had a hard time forgetting that. It was almost like those Tyler sisters had somehow become his to protect.

His and his brothers.

Matt knew the truth—he *was* a protector type.

He needed to keep those around him safe. And it was hard not to go overboard with Pip, even though she was a perfectly competent, capable woman.

He just wanted to be the one to protect her. Her, specifically. Because Pip had stuck with him for months now.

He knew Levi felt the same with their house-keeper. It was hard to miss how Levi watched over Pan like a mother duck with only one duckling. It was starting to drive Pan nuts, but Matt and Nate found it amusing at times.

Levi had never met a woman he couldn't charm when he wanted. Except this one.

Pan didn't have a clue how his brother felt.

Rather like Pip had no idea how Matt felt about her. It was hard not to want to protect them; there was something about the entire family that made him feel that way. Him, Levi, Joel—and he suspected Nate, though his most contrary brother wouldn't dream of admitting it.

Joel had practically taken every one of Pip's siblings under his own wing.

Nate just tolerated them, though Matt knew his younger brother mostly had a problem with Pip's twin.

Nate sure pampered Phoebe, though. He went out of his way for their sister-in-law. Protective of her.

Hell, they all were.

Phoebe was fast becoming the center of their entire house, and they all knew it.

She was the first wife any of them had ever had. That made her damned special to all of them. It was hard not to go overboard with her.

And since Pan had moved in, well, Levi had already made it clear how he felt—even if Pan had no real idea. Yet. It was just a matter of time. Made it hard not to treat her like a baby sister.

It was Pip's face he saw in his dreams at night. Pip and that damned flood. The fear. The courage. The determination to save her sister, no matter what the cost.

But Pip didn't have a clue.

Matt didn't know how to change that without running her off completely.

11

Pip got her first look at the horse after Matt shifted out of her way. She was a beautiful creature. A cream buckskin; a small one. Delicate, feminine.

Frightened. Half-starved. And very, very pregnant.

Whatever had happened to this beautiful girl had left its mark on the horse's soul.

Pip didn't even know her name.

She kept her manner unthreatening, her tone soft. Her eyes met the horse's. "Hello, beautiful girl."

The wind kicked up outside the trailer. It would storm soon. Pip could smell the rain coming. So could the horse. The mare shook her head as a breeze blew through the trailer. "Do you feel that? The rain, the wind?" She stepped closer.

The animal tensed, her fear of everything new almost palpable on the air.

"Yes. You smell the world and you wonder where you'll go in it, don't you, baby? If you'll ever go anywhere, do anything at all in it. You wonder at your place in it. A part of you just wants a safe place to hide out in forever. But we both know the world doesn't spin that way."

Pip didn't know where the words came from; she just kept talking as the beautiful girl began to relax. A little. The fear would always be there. But the panic was receding. Pip just kept talking.

"We have to keep taking the next step. Maybe you see it, too. Someone makes you take that first step, and then it's a fenced pasture. Safety. But a cage, still. With the real world just on the other side of that fence. Waiting. You can't always hide from the world, baby. We have to do this. Come with me, sweetheart. We'll do the pasture first. With the big, scary men right outside. They're not so bad. I promise. Then we'll fly together."

12

MATT HEARD HER CROONING TO THE HORSE, heard the words she said. The rescue driver respectfully looked away. Neither man said anything about the emotion they heard in the woman's voice. How could they?

Matt hadn't had such a glimpse into a woman's soul like that in a long time. Did she realize what she was revealing to him? Did she even realize he could hear her?

Somehow, he doubted.

It took another half an hour of her crooning to the horse before she and the buckskin mare emerged.

Giving Matt his first real clear look at the horse.

He bit back a curse, seeing the abuse and the fear right there.

But the animal was walking docilely with Pip.

"Honey, can you get her down the ramp?"

"Should be able to." Pip kept her tone slow and hushed. For the horse's sake.

But his gut tightened anyway when she looked over her shoulder toward him. She'd taken her hat off. Without it she really couldn't hide that easily. Her fire-touched long hair was braided, but it was starting to loosen.

But it was the blue eyes that caught a man. Stuck with a man for a long, long time.

Made Matt's gut tighten in a way it hadn't in quite a while before he'd met her.

He forced himself to focus on the horse. The mare was going to need quite a lot of care. And if she was skittish of all men, there were going to be problems. He had one female vet tech, and she only worked weekends part-time.

It was only Tuesday. They needed to come up with another solution—and fast.

"What's her current medical condition?" he asked the driver from the rescue.

"She's stable, healthwise. No underlying problems, just needs some good food and a steady hand. Someone who can love her. A woman that can love her." The driver was a man about Matt's own age, and had a healthy appreciation in his eyes for the redhead currently leading the horse down the ramp. "Bet that one will do real good. That your wife?"

Matt hesitated. He looked at the woman in question. The sun had turned her hair to dark fire, a stark contrast to the cream horse with black points next to her.

They were both gorgeous. And he wasn't the only one who'd noticed. There was a handful of other people across the street, watching. Mostly men. Watching her. Did Pip even realize?

Even that damned director Rowland Bowles was staring at her and the mare. Matt wanted to shout from the rooftops that Pip Tyler was off limits.

That she was his.

"No. She's not my wife." Matt shifted slightly, putting his body in the man's line of sight.

The driver got the message. "I see. Very pretty lady. Well, I need to get back to where I came from. I need you to sign for receipt of her."

"What's her name?"

"She didn't have one. Previous owner just called her Horse. Guy had a sick sense of humor." The driver's tone told Matt exactly how the other man felt about the previous owner.

Matt looked at the horse. "Apparently. Thanks."

"No problem. Just glad to see she's in good hands. Smaller than we anticipated, but good ones."

"Pip Tyler's one of the best with horses I've ever seen. You should see her ride. Flies like the wind. The wind just loves her."

"I'll bet it does."

Pip was walking the horse around the space, crooning encouragement. Matt took the opportunity to study the animal more closely. "When she due to foal?"

"Within the month. We shouldn't have moved her, but we didn't have much choice. We just found her last week and don't have the space."

"We'll see she's taken care of," Matt promised. The pregnancy was a complication he hadn't been aware of. He'd have to get the horse settled someplace warm and safe quickly. Matt watched the trailer pull away, then closed the gate himself.

After the driver left, Matt stood and watched the woman and the horse. It was hard to miss the signs of the horse's pregnancy. Or how timid and frightened the small mare was.

But she was responding to Pip. He'd yet to see a horse that wouldn't.

Pip finally released her hold on the horse when the mare lost interest in the woman and found a nibble of grass more tempting.

Pip joined him at the fence. They turned and watched the mare. "What's going to happen to her?"

"I don't know yet. The sonofabitch hadn't even bothered to give her a name, honey. All I got on her is that file." And it wasn't very thick. He'd seen it before—the rescue sometimes just had to work with what they got and pray for the best in some cases. It would always anger him, though. Abuse always would.

"She needs a name. At least some kind of identity. How old is she? Three?"

"Closer to two, I think." He checked the file quickly. The horse was just a few months beyond her second birthday.

"A bit too young to be a mama."

"Yes. She'll probably not grow as large as an adult because of it. I've seen it before."

"She's rather large; you think it's twins?"

"I'll check the files. I don't think she'll let me do too thorough of an exam. The rescue has never sent me a seriously unhealthy horse, though. I think she just needs—"

"Safety."

He'd been going to say love. But to Pip fear was the biggest motivator, wasn't it?

"Look at her. She's enjoying the wind." She laughed lightly after she said it. Matt closed his eyes for a moment and just tried to breathe her in. Tried not to act like an idiot over the woman next to him.

"From what I was told she spent most of her time in a dark barn."

"No more. What are you going to do with her?" She looked up at him out of those blue eyes that made him feel like the center of her world in that instant.

Pip wanted the horse. Matt could see it in her eyes. But she would never ask. "I was going to ask you the same thing."

The words had just popped out, but when blue eyes looked up at him and widened he knew he was making the right choice. Hell, he didn't need another horse or foal. He had a strict plan in mind for his own horse operation. This little girl, he estimated she was barely thirteen and a half hands tall, didn't fit that plan. But the animal was a quarter horse.

Pip was raising quarter horses. Damned fine ones she'd trained as cutters. He'd purchased two geldings to use for that very purpose—not for breeding.

The horse's foal would help Pip regain the strides she'd lost when she'd been forced to sell to him a few months back. Especially if it was a filly.

And he'd give her more than just a horse if she'd let him. He'd give her just about everything he could. Everything he had.

"You heard me. She is going to take too much time for me to gentle her now. I just don't have it. Not that you do, but hell, Pip, I'm stuck out on calls all day. She needs frequent attention during the day. I just can't do it." A lie. They had plenty of hands on his family's ranch. It was one of the largest spreads in the county, after all. If he wanted the horse taken care of, he had people who could do it. He just...Pip wanted the mare, and he knew it. "Take the horse. And the foal. Resocialize her. We'll talk about what to do with her later."

"I..."

"It's not charity. At least not for you. But for her. She needs a chance, honey. A place to see that life doesn't have to be all fear." He brushed a hand down her cheek, moving the tendril of loose hair off her cheek and tucking it behind her ear. Pip had small ears and wore the tiniest little diamond stud in each one. "I can't think of a better place for Wind Lover than at the Tyler ranch."

13

HE'D ALWAYS BEEN FASCINATED BY HORSES—
but not enough to actually get near one of the
beasts. Rowland had always hated feeling like a
coward, though. He watched the yellow horse
being unloaded and felt like exactly that when he
realized the person in charge of the big creature
was none other than that teeny tiny redhead. Pip?
Was that right?

Rowland studied her quickly. She was identical to the other one, wasn't she? Though this one
had on an obviously old T-shirt and had her hair
braided down her back. She wasn't ugly—she
wasn't even plain—she just didn't play up her
assets.

This woman didn't wear makeup or paint her nails or dress to catch a man's attention at all.

Rowland had to admit that some women didn't need to. This was probably one of them. She wasn't the woman he wanted. Still, Rowland was a man, and a straight one at that. It had been a long time since he'd been with a woman. A long time.

Would this Pip be the type for long, slow loving? Gently treated, like Matt Masterson obviously was treating her now?

Rowland watched the two as they stood with the horse for the longest time. Masterson leaned closer to her whenever she spoke. Was it because she was that soft-spoken or because he was overeager to catch everything the woman said? Was that behind why Masterson had given his not-quite-friendly warning earlier, reminding Rowland not to overwhelm and upset the girl?

How did she feel about Big Bubba hovering over her?

Rowland had a much harder time figuring out the answer to that question.

But his writer's mind could imagine.

14

It took some doing, but they managed to get the horse Matt was now calling Wind Lover into the vet clinic's trailer and out to Pip's barn. They had three barns on the place. The one in the best repair was where her horse Air Dancer ruled supreme, along with Perci's Wind Dancer. Pan and Phoebe had taken Sky Dancer and Cloud Dancer with them when they'd relocated to the Masterson place. But it wasn't there that Wind Lover would be the most comfortable. Not with all those males hanging around, demanding her attention.

She settled the horse in the small, three-stall barn that had been on the property for more than two generations. It was old and somewhat shabby, but Wind Lover would be safe, warm, and dry. The middle barn held three horses that they boarded for people in town. That money went a long way to buying feed for Phoebe's little drove of goats.

Pip spent hours with little Wind Lover, getting the horse settled, learning her, letting her just feel Pip nearby.

Patient, loving.

Determined to win her trust.

It was going to take her time.

The horse needed to heal first.

She spent most of the next afternoon with Wind Lover, and she saw some real progress. The horse seemed to understand that Pip wasn't going to hurt her at all. She'd just finished cleaning the stall next to Wind Lover's when her arm caught on an exposed nail.

She tried to clean up the wound herself, but it wasn't happening. She needed an extra pair of hands. Perci should be around the place somewhere.

"Perci? Come help me for a minute." Pip called when she heard the sound of footsteps just inside the barn. She turned, expecting to see her sister. It wasn't her twin standing there. No; it was a big, tall, strong man. For a moment Pip fought panic, until she looked into the familiar blue eyes.

Matt.

Some of the tension filling her dissipated. Some, not all.

She was practically half-naked in front of him, after all. She clutched her shirt closer, attempting to cover the old bra she wore. There was no time to slip the shirt back over her head, not without him seeing more than she wanted to reveal. She forced herself to take a deep breath, to remember that Matt had never hurt her. Never would. She knew that. Intellectually. Emotionally? She was still a messed-up tangle of nerves. Stupid nerves. "What are you doing here?"

"I came to check on Wind Lover."

"I cut my arm, I was trying to take care of it. Just give me a second to put my shirt back on." She shouldn't have said anything about it. It was like she'd triggered his reaction. His eyes took the expected path—he looked down, to where she clutched the orange flannel close.

Pip might not be overly experienced, but she'd certainly seen appreciation like that in a man's eyes before. And Joel looked at Phoebe that way all the time. With just that same amount of heat. That hunger.

She swallowed as her mouth went dry. Matt had never looked at her that way before, had he?

Matt Masterson liked what he saw. And she strongly suspected he wanted to see more.

For one wild moment Pip wanted to just let go of the shirt and let him see. Let him see all of her that he wanted.

She wished she could. Wished she could be like Perci or Phoebe and trust enough to just let go with a man.

Her arms tightened on the material, instead.

Pip fought the shiver that went through her. For the first time, she wasn't shivering from fear. Or from cold. But from something that felt a little like heat, anticipation.

Because she *wanted* him to see.

She liked that he liked what he saw, didn't she? "Matt? A little privacy, please?" Before she ended up making a total fool of herself. He stepped out of the stall, and she hurriedly slipped the now ripped orange flannel back on, her fingers flying over the buttons.

She joined him outside of the stall. His eyes immediately went to the buttons of her shirt. "You missed one. I'd love to help you fix it, if you'd let me."

"I..." She didn't know how to flirt with a man. Or how to respond to one who was so...so...like Matt. "Why are you here again?"

"To check on the horse, remember?" He smiled at her, melting her insides. And then his eyes shifted a bit. To the arm she'd injured. "Honey, you're bleeding. Do you have a first-aid kit in here? I am a doctor, after all."

"Of horses and dogs, not of people."

"I still know how to use a Band-Aid, Pip. And I won't even peek, any more than I already have."

She didn't see where she had any choice. Pip handed him the first-aid kit and he made quick work of the two-inch gash on her arm. "I caught my arm on a nail."

"It's nasty, but I don't think it'll need stitches. If you want, I'll drive you into town. We can swing by the hospital and have Nate take care of it."

"I don't really think that's necessary." And

they didn't need another ER bill, not for a little cut like this. At most, she'd just wait until Perci came home and let her twin take care of it. Perci had stitched them all up before. It came in handy, having a sister who was a nurse.

"You're up-to-date on your tetanus?"

"I think so. I'm not sure, though." She appreciated how calm and matter-of-fact he was. No teasing, no pushing the boundaries. Just Matt. Always just Matt. Pip finally felt herself start to relax. It was always like this with him, wasn't it? Tense and afraid, then finally, that moment when she relaxed enough to be comfortable with him.

To forget the fear that had coated her life for so long and just *be* with him.

"I'll call Nate; have him send a booster home with your sister."

"I...that's not necessary, Matt. I can take care of myself."

"Why should you have to do it all alone? Sometimes, baby, a man just wants to take care of a woman. Makes him feel strong and worth something, makes him think he matters. To take care of the people he cares about." He brushed a finger over the fresh bandage. He let that finger dip lower, ghosting over the skin of her arm. "And I do care about you—a great deal, Philippa Tyler. Far more than you realize."

Pip fought a shiver at the unexpected touch.

Matt had really big hands. Hands that knew exactly how to touch, probably.

Pip didn't know what to say about that, so she said nothing at all. He turned the conversation back to Wind Lover, and she let him.

Pip didn't know how to deal with an attractive man. Period. Especially one who had hinted repeatedly that he found her attractive, as well.

Three months ago, it never would have occurred to her that a man like him would look at her that way. Matt had not stopped watching her from the moment he'd stepped into the barn.

Pip had never been so confused in her adult life as she was in that very moment.

For the first time in four years, she found a man attractive. And she didn't have a clue what to do about it. So Pip talked—about the horse and about the boys, and anything that popped up. They just talked, as she dealt with Wind Lover and he examined the mare.

She didn't know where the words came from, but she didn't miss the pleasure in those blue eyes of his.

Matt had beautiful eyes; he was the only brother to have blue eyes. She'd thought about his eyes often. More often than she wanted to think about.

She thought about *Matt* more often than she wanted to think about, too. Pip didn't have a clue what it meant.

15

Rowland was starting to see outwitting Matt Masterson as a real challenge. He'd recognized the big black truck in front of the Tylers' front porch, even without *Masterson Vet Clinic* on the side. Still, as long as Masterson didn't want Rowland's redhead, then he could tolerate having the man around, right? There were two redheads available, not like each man couldn't have the one they wanted.

Besides, Rowland had made a point of never sleeping with a woman he wanted to work with—or did work with—that was just irresponsible, after all.

Men like Matt Masterson were enough to

make other men feel weak and pitiful. Not Rowland, of course, but other men. Less confident men. Masterson walked at the side of the quieter redhead again as they came from a small barn near the rear of the pasture.

Rowland would bet good money the two of them had a real thing going between them, though people he'd asked in town hadn't heard such.

No, but the town had been full of wild speculation about the mysterious Tyler sisters—who had apparently just appeared out of nowhere three months earlier when their eldest sister had snagged the attention of one of Masterson County's most eligible bachelors.

Not everyone in town was too pleased with it.

He'd found it intriguing and filed the story away in his mental files for when he someday got the urge to write another romantic film.

Romance wasn't exactly something he understood a lot about.

The redhead stopped walking—and talking—when she saw Rowland. Masterson put a hand on her back, almost as if he was supporting her. Masterson glowered at Rowland.

What a quiet little timid ragamuffin she was,

needing the big strong cowboy at her side to keep her safe.

Rowland fought a snort.

"Bowles, why are you here?"

"Someone mentioned I might want to consider the Tyler ranch for one of my locations. I figured I'd take a look today." Bullshit, but now that he was here he could see where the run-down ranch had real potential as Keith's place. Keith was a secondary character in his latest project. The hero's closest friend, an honorable, hard-working rancher who didn't believe in magic or mysticism at all. He'd inherited a struggling ranch that was a portal to a mystical realm that only Gretta could open. Keith would eventually end up as guardian to all the witch fairies who crossed through that portal. Keith was a natural guardian.

Much like Matt Masterson probably was.

The Tyler ranch was ragged, so he wouldn't have to spend any money making it look run-down, and then fix it back up when he was finished. He'd done that a fair time or two before. It could get expensive.

No, the Tyler ranch *was* run-down. He winced. Money certainly was tight, wasn't it? Well, that could work in his favor.

And there were children running around. Boy children, chickens, ducks, and—heaven help him —goats, running everywhere. He didn't think any of the Tyler sisters were old enough to have pre-teens, but...maybe they were older than they looked?

"My father is the one who makes those kinds of decisions, Mr. Bowles, and he's in Texas for a few more weeks. I'm afraid you'll have to look elsewhere," the girl said. She turned toward the boys. "Pete, get your things together. I'm taking you three over to Phoebe's for dinner tonight."

Rowland didn't miss the pleasure that rushed across Masterson's face as the vet spoke. Masterson was pitiful. Absolutely pitiful.

"I didn't know that."

"Perci and I need to speak with Phoebe and Pan tonight. Family things," she said quietly. "Joel's going to hang out with the boys."

"You're staying for dinner, too?" Masterson practically wheedled the question.

Rowland snorted silently. Didn't the man have any pride?

Or was there more to this Tyler sister than met the eye?

What was it about her that drew a man like

Masterson's attention when her identical sister was just as beautiful yet ten times more confident as a woman?

What was it about Pip Tyler that this Masterson was so hung up on?

"Yes."

"Good. Then I'll drive you and the boys over. I'll even give you a lift back."

"That's not—"

"I know. But I want to, ok?"

Yeah, Masterson was in pursuit. Did the Tyler woman even know it? He was interested in watching how it played out. For research purposes only, of course.

And how was that going to interfere with what Rowland wanted?

He was about to ask another question, anything to get her attention onto him and not on Masterson or the small kid yanking on her shirt making demands, when a twenty-something-year-old Chevy pulled in the drive.

The redhead he'd truly come to see parked and stepped out. She approached the front porch where they waited with wariness on her beautiful face.

She looked exhausted—and it was only six in

the evening. Long day at the hospital, most likely. She was going to work herself to an early grave, just like half the people he'd met in small places like this that were barely struggling to make it day by day.

Her and her pretty twin both. What a waste.

"Famous movie director Rowland Bowles on Tyler property. What are the odds?" she said, shooting her sister a significant look. The raga-muffin shrugged quietly. Always quiet, that one, wasn't she? "What can we do for you tonight?"

"I came to look at your property to use as a po-tential location. And to see you and your twin. Rumor has it the two of you are breathtakingly beautiful and would look awe inspiring on the big screen."

"Pip would. I'm too mean for breathtaking. I'd make a good villain, though. Just ask Masterson's brother Nate." She handed her bag to one of her brothers and the kid didn't hesitate to carry it inside for her. "So what's the real reason a famous movie director showed up here today? What do you want?"

Her twin said something quietly behind her, but Rowland had almost forgotten the twin was even there. Something about the way Perci Tyler stared at a man, it was enough to have him forgetting his true purpose.

"I need a Gretta." He realized how stupid he sounded and tried again. "I have a role that I need to fill. I like to use locals whenever possible. You have the look I want. And I saw you...on your horse a week or so back. You looked exactly how I expected Gretta would. I'm willing to pay you, of course."

She smiled mysteriously at him. As if she knew a joke. "Saw me on my horse, you say? When was this?"

"Six nights ago. On the Masterson ranch. Riding a big red monster."

"I see." She shot a look over at her twin then smiled mysteriously. "You sure about that?"

"Certain." Wasn't he?

"Hmmm. I'm not interested right now. And even if I was, I have a packed schedule at the hospital. There is no way Dr. Beelzebub Masterson would ever let me have time off to make a movie. I'm sorry. You'll have to find your Gretta elsewhere."

"I'm talking serious money. Everyone told me today that any money will help your family. Think about it. It can change your life, being in one of my films. It's happened before."

"Oh, I'm sure it has. But I'll tell you again, Bowles. I'm not the woman you want."

Matt Masterson coughed behind him. Rowland fought turning around to see the man laughing at the nurse's rejection of his offer. Let Masterson laugh and think it was funny, then. Rowland didn't care.

Oh, well. Rowland wasn't the type to give up easily.

16

MATT SPENT MOST OF THE NEXT DAY thinking about what Rowland Bowles had offered him and his brothers to use their ranch. It was a substantial cash offer. Not needed, but it certainly wouldn't hurt. His share would be enough to buy out his brothers on the third ranch they'd purchased under Levi's direction. It had once been a great-uncle's place. They'd made a plan five years ago to buy back all the original Masterson land that they could.

Matt was using it to run his horse operation. Once he got things up and running, he'd even be able to operate a satellite vet office out there and board patients if he needed.

It meant dealing with Bowles, though.

"Well, I think Bowles is an idiot," Matt heard his housekeeper say hotly as the door opened late the next afternoon. No surprise, his housekeeper had a bit of a temper at times. Like her older sister Perci—and like his sister-in-law Phoebe. The only Tyler sister that didn't seem quick to anger was Pip. "It's obvious that it wasn't Perci out there that night. I mean, they're identical. Not like most people can tell them apart. Ninety percent of our own family can't tell them apart."

Matt's attention sharpened; he leaned back in his desk chair—closer to the open door. Sometimes having a home office right next to the front door had real advantages.

He'd known who they were speaking of the moment they'd mentioned identical. And Bowles.

Matt agreed with Pan's assessment. The guy was an idiot if he couldn't see that it had been Pip out there that night. Everyone seemed to realize that except for Bowles.

"How much of it is him seeing what he expects to see—and how much is it Pip keeping him from seeing her? We both know she hides from men, especially big men like Bowles," Phoebe said, her tones those of a woman who'd been deaf for years. Matt settled back in his office chair as he listened to the sounds of women in his house.

It had been him and his three brothers living together since Matt was not any older than his twenty-two-year-old housekeeper. His mother had a place three miles from town that she used on her rare returns to Masterson County. She hadn't stayed in town much after his father's death and Nate taking over the hospital admin for her shortly after. That had been well over a year ago.

She said Masterson hurt too much without their father.

Women like Phoebe and her youngest sister Pan were completely foreign to this ranch. Matt liked that that was changing.

He was starting to get used to having Pan around. She was very good at her job—running their house, while her sister was back at the Tyler ranch each day. It was hard not to think of her as a baby sister already.

Pan, like all the rest of those Tyler redheads, brought out protective urges in a man. Matt wouldn't deny it.

It was the mention of that damned director, Bowles, that truly caught his attention, though. Joel and Nate had shoved the moron on to Matt, damn them. And Matt knew the director was enjoying getting right under Matt's skin. It was almost like the guy was getting a kick out of pushing his buttons whenever he could.

"Pan? Everything ok?" He'd seen her talking to Rowland Bowles when the man had stopped by to pester Levi into letting him use the spread for some scenes that morning before Matt had taken off to the northern corner of the county to tend to a herd of sick cattle.

Pan and Phoebe looked at him out of identical blue eyes, and similar sweet faces. They were beautiful young women, that was for sure. As were the twins. When the four of them were standing next to each other, a man had trouble breathing. It just was. And had been from the moment he'd first seen the Tyler sisters.

At least it was for Matt. And Joel. And Levi. And he suspected, Nate.

If Nate would ever just admit it.

They'd lived less than ten miles past his place for their entire lives and he'd never known they'd existed. Until the day he'd answered Pip's advertisement for some AQH cutting horses, on Levi's behalf.

Pip.

Matt felt a smile curve his lips when he remembered how the sun had shown through her hair, how she had turned to look at him as she climbed off the big gelding that was almost the exact shade of mahogany as her hair. She'd asked which one of them was Matt. She had walked right up to him. Looked right at him like she knew. He'd been damned glad to be Matt that day.

He'd been captivated by her ever since. Her sisters were beautiful, but Pip was more than that. And he knew why he felt that way. Why he had practically from the beginning.

"Bowles showed up again at the ranch. He wants Perci in his movie and he's determined. He's convinced it was her he saw. And says she's perfect for some mythical lost fairy character he has. Which is ridiculous," Pan said, hotly.

"I know. It was Pip he saw. I saw her ride that night, too. And she did look like a fairy or a pixie." A thought occurred to him. "He's not harassing them, is he? I can talk to him."

"Thanks, Matt. But we Tylers can handle an idiot like Rowland Bowles," Pan said. "He'll get the message eventually, and just go away. Perci's giving him the runaround as much as possible, too. I think she's enjoying it. It's up to Pip if we ever tell him the truth. And she hasn't decided yet. We talked to Dad about the film crew. He wants to think about it for a while."

"Just let me know if Bowles gets to be too annoying. Apparently the town has assigned Bowles to the Mastersons for the time being, and my brothers gave him to me. We're supposed to make him feel welcome or something."

And if Bowles caused Pip one moment of anxiety or upset or embarrassment, Matt would take care of it. He'd warned the man to stay away from the Tylers.

Apparently, Bowles had trouble listening.

17

JAY TOOK HIS TIME. THE TYLER RANCH WAS
empty for the night; he'd driven along behind
them on the highway as they'd pulled into the
Masterson ranch.

Damned Mastersons had bought up every
struggling ranch between their old family homestead and the Tylers' place. Taking over. Surrounding them.

Like they'd planned it that way.

No surprise; he'd heard the rumors that at
least one of Pip's sisters was going around with
one of the sheriff's brothers.

Jay took the opportunity to poke around Pip's

place, see what it was the girl he was going to marry liked. It was easy to figure out which room was hers—the bitch twin had a drawer full of hospital scrubs.

Pip had serviceable flannel and cotton shirts and jeans. Stuff a real ranch woman needed.

She'd be a big help to him running his ranch, wouldn't she? When she wasn't inside, raising his boys, that was.

There was a pregnant mare in the barn he'd seen his Pip come out of that afternoon. Jay tried to make friends with the buckskin, but she wasn't the friendly sort. He saw the scars on her side from a whip and knew it had to be the horse that damned Masterson had given her.

Rumors were easy to hear in Masterson County, after all.

The entire town was talking about how the vet had just given one of the Tyler sisters a buckskin mare worth quite a bit of cash. Just given the mare to her as a present.

This had to be her. Jay had to admit she was a beautiful animal, and he could see where she would appeal to a small thing like his Pip. Small and gentle, just the right size for a woman like Pip.

He'd have to make room for the mare in his own barn, wouldn't he?

Her and the foal.

Because that would make Pip happy.

That was all Jay wanted, after all.

18

MATT DROVE THE TEN OR SO MILES BETWEEN his place and the Tyler ranch probably a bit faster than he should have. Especially as he neared Wreck Road Curve, an area known for the most collisions in the county. He'd learned that one of the wooden crosses perched high above the curve represented Pip's mother. He hadn't forgotten that. He forced himself to slow down.

Horses foaled normally at least ninety percent of the time. Just because Pip had sounded worried and scared when she'd called him didn't mean something was wrong.

Or that he had to rush over there like a crazy moron. Pip had bred horses since she was sixteen,

Phoebe had told him. That was remarkable in it-self. Pip knew what she was doing.

Still, Pip needed him. He wanted to be right there as quickly as he could. Especially at a quarter after midnight.

Matt had it bad for that woman and he knew it. The porch light was on when he pulled into the Tyler ranch. He didn't bother going to the door. For one thing, it was far too late, and he didn't want to wake the kids sleeping inside. For another, he knew exactly where Pip was. He rounded the house and headed to the small barn a hundred yards away from the house. There were two other barns on the property, but Matt knew she had iso-lated Wind Lover, keeping her away from the stal-lions and geldings who would have frightened the mare.

Pip hadn't wanted to stress the new mother as her time had neared. She had the barn door open, and Matt called out softly when he approached. Pip was just as skittish as the horse and he knew it. A man coming up on her unexpectedly in the middle of the night would terrify her.

"Baby, how is she?" Pip was dressed in a soft pair of pajama pants and a thin little tank top. That hair of hers was down around her shoulders, making a man's fingers curl to touch. But now was not the time. With one look at the horse, he knew that they weren't going anywhere tonight. Wind Lover was foaling, and it was a bit early. At least by his estimation.

"She's been walking into position. I don't think it'll be long, but she's terribly frightened." Pip brushed the hair out of her eyes quickly, causing the thin dark cotton of her shirt to stretch over her chest. Matt was a total idiot over this woman, and he knew it. He should be focused on the horse and not on her. But it was so damned hard to do.

"Let's take a look; see what we've got going on here."

"We usually use Dr. Murphy. But I thought... since it was her...that you needed to be here, too."

"Anytime you need me, baby, I'm going to be here. All you have to do is call."

It took longer than Pip expected for the foal to make her way into the world. As the hours passed, she found herself sitting next to the man and just talking. About anything. More than she'd spoken with anyone other than her family in a long time.

Matt was full of stories of horses and animals and vet school. She had her own stories—mostly of her sisters and their misadventures—and Matt actually listened. Cared what she had to say.

As they relaxed with each other, the horse seemed to calm a little, too.

Matt shocked her when he started crooning old country-gospel songs to the mare. Pip smiled as she settled on the old saddle blanket Matt had grabbed and spread over a pile of hay in one corner.

Matt settled down right next to her; she could feel his warmth pressed up against her. As she listened to him sing, her eyes drifted closed and Pip relaxed. Until sleep finally caught up with her and she snuggled into the strong male arms around her.

19

Being an identical twin meant always having a part of yourself out there somewhere. It wasn't any different for Perci. Plus, she'd shared a room with her twin from the moment they'd been born. They practically breathed in sync sometimes.

Pip wasn't where she was supposed to be. Perci knew that before she even set foot in the house.

Pip was outside. Somewhere.

There were only a handful of real possibilities —and one was the most likely.

Knowing Pip, she was in the barn, surrounded by the horses that were her sister's lifeblood. For her to be out there at four in the morning, though, something had to be wrong.

When Perci entered the far barn, there was a light glowing near the south end. Wind Lover, the little buckskin Matt had rescued, then.

It was always those damned Mastersons causing trouble, wasn't it?

Perci's lip curled when she thought of the altercation she'd had that afternoon with the great Nate. It still burned her almost twelve hours later. If he wasn't her boss, she'd probably have kicked that devil in the...

For a moment when she first saw the long, tall muscled man curled on the hay next to her twin, she thought it was Nate. Thought it was Nate holding Pip so close.

A weird rush of something not so pleasant went straight through her.

Until she realized the Masterson holding her sister like he cared was Matt. One of the nice ones. The quietest brother who had a touch of gold with animals of all kinds. Calm, quiet, gentle, kind—he was the brother who kept to himself most of all.

Figured he'd be the one Pip would feel safe enough to sleep next to.

That's when it hit her. After everything that had happened to her sister when they'd been nineteen—an event that still made Perci feel as guilty as hell when she thought about it—Pip felt safe enough to sleep next to a man. Any man.

That was a real milestone for Pip. One Perci had thought would never happen. It had tears streaming down Perci's cheeks as she gave a prayer of thanks.

Fitting that it would be the quiet brother who'd gotten to her sister.

They looked very pretty together—Pip so small and beautiful, him so strong and rugged.

Perci started to back away from where they slept. She bumped into someone standing behind her. She turned to see her father. He must have gotten home from his most recent visit to Texas. He held his fingers to his lips and nodded.

Perci followed him out of the barn. She didn't speak until they were back inside the house where the rest of her siblings slept. "She trusts him."

"On some level, she does." Her father handed her a piece of freshly baked bread that Pip had most likely made that afternoon, and the jar of jam they'd put up the previous season. "I am both glad of it—"

"And worried," Perci sighed. "Another damned Masterson? All we need is for Pan and one of the other two—"

"Pan is still young." Her father leveled a look at her. "Levi Masterson looks at her when she's not watching. He'll make his move one of these days. That in the barn surprises me, though."

"Does it? She's always said horses were the best judge of man. He's got a way with them. And apparently a way with her." He'd probably gentled her just like Pip had broken through to that little buckskin outside. The parallels weren't lost to Perci.

"But I don't think she realizes it yet. I figured he'd take more time with her. Not rush her so much."

"And that is what has you worried."

He leveled a serious look at her. "When a man looks at a woman that way, any father will worry. And Perci...Nate Masterson does some looking of his own. I figured it would be you first. Before Pip. Or Pan for that matter, though with her right over there with Levi, I wonder."

"Not going to happen—he's going to be looking at a dirt clod if he keeps coming at me like he does. He despises me. And that's all there is to it."

"Does he? Let me ask you this; are you prepared for him to be a bigger part of your life than what he is? Because thanks to your sister—and possibly the other two—that doctor of yours is going to be around for the rest of your lives. Better make your peace with him sooner rather than later. I'm going to bed. Now that I know where the two of you are, and that you are both safe, I can rest now. It's been a long week. I'm taking a blood sample back to Texas in the morning, for Worthington-Deane to have analyzed. I'm getting too old for all of this traveling. Love you, baby girl. You and your brothers and sisters."

Perci had a lot going through her mind—it was a long time before she was able to sleep.

Nate Masterson was the last man she would ever want in her life. But that was apparently right where he was going to be.

20

MATT KNEW THE MOMENT SHE WOKE. SHE was almost like a little cat, stretching and snuggling. He stroked a hand down her spine and tried to ignore the feel of small breasts pressing into his ribs, of soft red hair brushing against his cheek. Of the thin leg thrown over his and her warmth pressed against him, almost right where a man wanted it.

He wanted this woman. Wanted her badly. He lay there for the longest time while watching the horse labor, just thinking about what he wanted from the woman he held.

A man getting involved with Pip would have to be in it for the long haul.

But would that be so bad? She was beautiful, smart, talented, kind, loving, and gentle. Loyal and brave. When she smiled at him he felt like a damned hero. Like he could slay her dragons and be her prince. Fanciful of him and made him feel like a damned idiot. But it was the truth.

Was this how Joel had felt with Pip's older sister? It explained a lot. How his brother had met her and practically fell for her right then and there. Joel had taken one look at her and was a goner.

Much like Matt had with his Pip.

Her small hand pressed against his chest, right over his heart, as those blue, blue eyes of hers popped open when the sun first shone through the open barn door. He saw the immediate fear and felt like a monster. "Shhh. It's ok. We just fell asleep. Nothing wrong with that. You're safe. We still don't have a foal yet, though."

The fear slipped away as clarity settled in. It had Matt wondering. What had happened to her to make her so frightened? And it had. There was a reason. "Why are you so afraid of me, honey? I'm never going to hurt you."

PIP WAS SILENT FOR A LONG MOMENT. WAS she afraid of Matt? To be honest, that was exactly what she was. Afraid. Of him, of Joel, and Nate, and every man that didn't share a blood relation with her—and half that did. She didn't want to be. Not any longer. That wasn't fair to her or to him. Matt had been nothing but kind to her from the moment they had met. "I'm not afraid. I'm not going to be anymore."

"Because of Gunderson. He did something to you, didn't he?"

She nodded. Sometimes it felt like her entire adulthood had been shaped by Jay Gunderson.

She hadn't always been quite this afraid, though she'd always been reserved and shy and a bit anxious over things.

Her anxiety had just gotten worse after Jay's attack, and after the night his father had shown up on their doorstep and threatened them all to just keep them quiet about what Jay had tried to do. After the night her mother had first been injured and she'd known before Gunderson had shown up again that Perci was in serious trouble.

Gunderson hadn't broken the news of the wreck kindly. He'd almost gotten enjoyment in telling them her family was hurt.

"Because of him. And what he tried to do. And because after...his father didn't want me saying anything about it. He showed up one day when it was just my sisters and me at home. He had to have been watching to see the rest of our family leave. We were nineteen, Pan was seventeen, and Phoebe twenty-one. When our mother died, it was Sheriff Gunderson again. And he blamed Phoenix because of me. To show he still had all the power, even though Jay was in jail before then."

Before she could say anything else, strong male hands wrapped around her waist. She was pulled over that ridiculously strong chest until her nose was practically touching his. "You did not cause Gunderson's actions, sweetheart. I don't want you thinking that. Clive Gunderson has been an asshole since egg met sperm. His boy has been just like him from the time he was created. He targeted your family because he was a bully. Period. If it hadn't been you he focused on, it would have been some other vulnerable young girl. Some other family his father could terrorize. Not you. No one could possibly blame *you* for anything that happened. Anything."

His hand buried itself in her hair and he

guided her head to rest on his shoulder. Pip just let him. What else could she do? A part of her was saying run. Another part was urging her to cuddle up closer to the first man to touch her since she'd been nineteen.

Matt would never hurt her. She knew that. Deep inside where it really mattered she knew that. Pip let him hold her for a really long time.

Until her eyes drifted closed once again.

21

Rage unlike any other Matt had ever felt threatened to choke him. How long had she been carrying this burden? Blaming herself for circumstances well beyond her control? Matt forced himself to remain as outwardly calm as possible. One wrong move, one wrong word, and she would bolt. He wasn't about to let that happen.

Not now. He kissed her lightly, just a quick brush against dark red curls. He wondered if she had even felt it. Her breathing evened out against his chest, and she unconsciously snuggled closer.

Matt's fate was sealed in that instant, and he knew it. She just fit right exactly where she was.

Matt wasn't about to let her go. Not any time soon. And not until he absolutely had to.

Matt held Pip, absurdly touched at seeing her small body curled there on the hay. The exhaustion she felt showed beneath her eyes and in the depth of her sleep. He thought about waking her or carrying her inside, putting her in her own bed where she belonged, but when Wind Lover whickered, he knew he couldn't do that. The two were so bonded the horse needed Pip nearby. And Pip would never forgive him if he took her inside. That left only one option. He pulled the spare blanket from the shelf and tossed it over her.

There was plenty of room left for him. He took advantage of it, sitting beside the woman and thinking for a very long time.

She didn't open her eyes again until he shook her awake just in time for them to watch Wind Lover bring her first filly into the world.

Matt just held her as they watched.

22

Matt's hands itched to touch her again, even three days later. Matt knew he was being ridiculous. A man's hands didn't really itch to touch a woman. Even a woman like Philippa Tyler.

Nor did a man really hum with anticipation that he'd get to see a woman again that night. Ridiculous. No matter which way he looked at it. Matt was a man of science; he understood how attraction worked.

He was attracted to Pip. More than just simply attracted. He found her far too intriguing for his own good.

He'd practically thought of nothing else since

the moment he'd held her in his arms in that shabby barn of hers. Held her, smelled her, felt her pressed against him in all the ways that a woman should be pressed against a man.

Matt tried to force himself to focus on the files in front of him, but all concentration fled when he heard female voices.

A lot of female voices. Voices Matt recognized. He stood and stepped toward his office door.

There she was. Dressed in a simple tank top and faded denims. Her hair was pulled up in a ponytail. Her cheeks were slightly sunburned. She looked perfectly kissable, touchable.

Damn it; his hands were itching, weren't they?

Matt smiled. "Ladies."

"Hi, Matt. The twins came over to get ready for the dance here. You still not going?" Pan asked.

He'd planned to stay home and go over some herd records, but all of that changed in an instant. When Pip turned to him and smiled shyly, Matt shook his head. It was simple, really, wasn't it? If Pip was going to the dance, then so was Matt. Period. "I'm going to have to dig deeper into my files, honey. It'll have to be done during business hours.

I'm going to head to the community center for a few hours, at least."

He'd stay there as long as Pip did. Simple as that.

"Good. That'll be all four of you, then," Phoebe smiled up at him. All the Tyler sisters had killer smiles that could knock a man back. Phoebe was no exception.

It was still Pip's shy smile that he'd dreamed about last night. Pip wearing that special smile and nothing else. "I'll head on up now. Get changed. You'll each save me a dance, right? Or do I need to get in line after those brothers of mine?" He grinned at Pip's twin. "Heard you're going with Nate, right? He's real excited, from what Levi said."

The expected response was right there. Just like he'd known it would be. The two of them would never get along.

Or they'd finally figure things out and end up burning the sheets together. Incinerating each other.

Perci's sisters teased her about Nate. It gave Matt a chance to slip up to Pip's side. He leaned down until he could speak softly to her. "How are Wind Lover and the baby? Named her yet?"

23

Pip looked up at the man next to her. Had he deliberately cut her off from her sisters? He was between her and them, strong and warm, and her fingers curled with the urge to touch the green shirt he wore, to see if it was as soft as it looked. See if the muscles beneath were as hard as they looked. "She's doing better. And I'm calling the baby Dream Dancer. She's beautiful, Matt. Seems healthy, too."

"Good. I'll be out tomorrow to check on her. You want to ride with me tonight? Joel's SUV will get mighty crowded with all of you in there."

For a moment a thrill of some kind went through her. A heat of some kind.

It took Pip a second to realize that she wanted his attention on her. All his attention, and only on her.

That way.

But that was stupid. Matt was a friend, nothing more. A friend, even a distant relative, maybe. He probably saw her the same way he obviously saw Pan and Perci. As Phoebe's little sisters.

That was all it was. She was being silly to think it was anything else.

Still, it wasn't Pan he'd singled out, cut off from the rest of her sisters. It was her. Why had he done that? It wasn't just about Wind Lover and the filly.

At least, she didn't think so. He was talking to her in that voice. The same one he used with the wounded horse.

Why was he doing that? Was he trying to coax her into something?

Maybe he just wanted a quiet moment or two to talk about Wind Lover? She was never going to be able to figure him out.

Pip found herself nodding before she thought about it. "Of course. I think we're leaving about seven. Perci and I were going to ride with Pan and Levi."

"Great. I'm going to go change clothes myself. You all planning to eat anywhere before the dance?"

"Pan mentioned Jasper's." The dance would have refreshments, but there was a tiny little truck stop just outside of town that they would go to occasionally. When they had the money. Jasper's was very affordable. And that was what mattered to their family. Money for eating out was very, very rare.

"Great. I think your sisters are waiting."

24

PERCI WATCHED PIP AND MATT AND KNEW her sister didn't have a clue how the man felt. Matt was into her sister in a very big way. Should she pull Pip aside and tell her twin? Or just let things fall naturally?

Another Masterson with her twin. Her twin. At times, it was like Pip was the other half of her, yet here was this man pulling her away. Perci didn't know how she felt about that.

Pip hadn't been involved with a man since she'd lost her virginity at eighteen then dated that guy for two months while they'd both been enrolled at the small community college sixty-five miles south of Masterson.

Pip had dropped out after that damned Gunderson monster hurt her. At a dance much like the one tonight.

Perci renewed her determination to stick close to her sisters tonight.

It was Pip's first dance since that night four years ago. She strongly suspected her twin was afraid. Perci could almost feel it on that weird twin channel they shared.

Pip didn't look afraid right now. She looked happy to be right where she was. Matt had almost surrounded her sister right there by the door of his home.

Perci thought about what a relationship with Matt Masterson would mean for her sister.

She didn't think Matt would just be messing around with Pip. Not unless he was serious in some way. It just didn't seem like something the quietest brother would do. She didn't think he'd hurt Pip, either. Because that would hurt Phoebe and Joel. And Matt just wouldn't do that.

So he had to be serious, right?

He wasn't the kind of guy to play around with a woman like Pip. He just wasn't.

So what would that mean for Pip in the long run?

Perci had heavy thoughts for the next hour and half as she and her sisters dug through the clothes they'd brought with them and figured out just what exactly they needed to wear. It had been a long time since they'd had such a fun afternoon, since they'd had an opportunity, really.

And for the first time in four years, Pip was right there with the rest of them, too.

Perci wondered how much of it was because of Matt Masterson and how much was because her sister was finally healing. Perci didn't have a clue.

25

Matt stayed by her side the entire time they were walking into the small dive he and his brothers had never bothered eating at before. The Tylers were apparently well known. It just went to show how they could have lived almost next door to the Tylers the women's entire lives and not know they existed.

They had traveled in completely different circles, apparently.

That was going to change.

Joel noticed Matt's interest first, and when he, Matt, and Nate were waiting at the counter to pick up their orders, Joel called him on it. "Staking a claim?"

Nate looked between the two of them. "Excuse me?"

"Not you. Matt. The wind blows in that direction?" Joel leveled a look at him. "It a serious one? Not that I don't trust you, but Phoebe freaks whenever her sisters are involved. Especially Pip. They are all extremely protective of her."

"Because of Gunderson. I know most of the story. Pip's told me."

Joel nodded. Matt saw the confusion on Nate's face.

Matt filled him in quietly. "Gunderson got pissed at Perci, took it out on Pip by assaulting her at a dance. From what I heard, Phoebe hit him over the head with a potted plant literally in the nick of time, and Pan kicked his dick into his throat, while Perci dealt with her twin."

"Shit. I wondered why they seem to overprotect her at times. Why Perci's almost rabid about knowing where her twin's at." Nate's eyes held compassion. "She going to be ok tonight?"

Joel paid the cashier and took the white bags of food for him. "To be honest, Phoebe's seriously worried. Pip's the sweet one of the four, apparently. The most vulnerable."

"Not any longer." On that, Matt was one hundred percent clear. He was going to be standing there between Pip and anything that threatened her ever again. She'd been quiet in the truck on the drive over, but he'd understood. She was nervous, trapped in the truck cab with him. He'd kept the conversation on Wind Lover as much as he could. Until she'd relaxed and was speaking more freely with him.

He was seducing her, using the mare and foal as a cover. But he was determined and would do what it took.

"Thought as much," Joel said.

"You serious about her? Don't think those girls are the kind a real man toys with." Nate threw a glance over his shoulder at the table where the four sisters and Levi waited. Matt followed his gaze. His brother and Pan were discussing something between them animatedly. No surprise. They were both business people at heart, and each had some wildly different theories on things. Plus, Levi, the biggest player of the Masterson brothers, had it bad for their housekeeper. And apparently didn't know what to do about it.

Matt empathized.

"Very serious. More serious than I've been about a woman in years." Matt knew his brothers understood his meaning when he continued. "I don't plan on letting her out of my sight tonight. If there are any problems, I plan to be there right next to her."

And he intended to start now.

PIP FORCED HERSELF NOT TO HYPERVENTILATE the closer Matt drove to the Masterson Community Center. She'd not been inside the center since that night four years ago. She had just not wanted to be there.

Her family had understood and hadn't pushed her. But tonight...

Phoebe had asked them to go. Had wanted everyone to show support for Joel after what had happened with Rutherford. Half the town had liked the man who had tried to kill them all, and some were questioning Joel's position as sheriff. It was Phoebe's way of daring those few people to say something to those who had paid the greatest cost for Rutherford's actions. The man could have killed Phoebe, Joel, Phoenix—even Pip, Perci, Matt, and Nate—with the way he'd been shooting at them all.

He'd cut up a squirrel and left it on their porch for her seven-year-old brother to find. When Phoebe had told her people were doubting that ever happened, Pip had had to force the anger back.

Parker would never forget that day. None of them would. Anyone who dared to question them, well, Pip had no problem telling them what she thought.

For her family, Pip would do just about anything. For her family.

"Heavy thoughts?" the man driving the truck asked. Pip looked over at him. Matt was a beautiful man, wasn't he? He was probably the most handsome of his brothers, though he wasn't the tallest. Nate was; Nate was huge and burly and the size of a small mountain.

Matt was six foot three or so, though, and very strong.

It was hard to miss. "I just don't always like crowds."

"I don't particularly, either."

"Phoebe wanted us all to go. Because of what people are saying about Joel." She wanted his opinion on what the town was saying. He was a part of the town in a way she and her family most definitely were not.

"What are they saying? I haven't heard anything."

"Someone is stirring up trouble for him, I think. Saying things like Tom Rutherford got a raw deal. That kind of stuff." Pip had a scar on her forehead. They'd first thought it was from hitting something in the floodwater that day. But she didn't remember that. She did remember something cutting her forehead right before Matt had lifted her over a rock when Rutherford had been shooting at them. "My scar. I think it's from a bullet."

Matt looked at her right eyebrow. "I know that it is. It's why I grabbed for you first instead of Phoebe that day. You were right in that bastard's line of fire. I watched it happen. Anyone says anything to you about Rutherford, you send them right to me. I'll tell them exactly what kind of deal he got. With the devil."

"I wish we knew where John Rutherford was." Tom Rutherford's younger brother had been in the wind for more than three months now. Pip was always aware that he was still out there somewhere. And Joel had killed his brother. Hard to forget that. She wouldn't, until the police had him.

"The state police will find him eventually. I don't doubt it. I get the first dance tonight, right?" He smiled at her, looking far too handsome in that moment for any woman's own good.

The Masterson brothers were some of the prettiest she'd ever seen. Maybe not all of them were handsome in the classical sense, but they were rugged, strong, masculine, and best of all —heroic.

Matt and Nate hadn't had to come out there to help her and Perci find Phoebe that day. But they had.

She'd tried to tell herself it was because of their brother.

But it had been her that Matt had covered with his own body that day. Her that he had dragged out of the river. And Phoebe. Nate had protected Perci, who had been tied to a tree and without real cover. Nate had covered her sister with his own body, too. Because he and his brothers were good men.

Not like Rutherford. Not like Gunderson.

"I don't know how to dance. Not really."

"I don't think many people in Masterson do.

But I wouldn't mind trying, with you. At least you won't laugh at me if I fall flat on my face." He grinned as he looked at her.

She couldn't imagine him ever falling flat on his face in anything. He was just too confident for that. "Of course not."

"Good."

Matt parked his truck next to his brother Levi's. "Stay there; I'll help you down."

She did. Not because she wasn't capable of climbing down by herself, but she was in heels. Something she wasn't used to. He opened the door and lifted her down to the gravel.

Pip wrapped her fingers around his strong arms and let him hold her. Just for a second.

Until Perci was at her elbow and it was time to go in.

The panic returned.

Warm fingers wrapped around hers. Pip looked over. Matt was holding her hand. Holding her close to his side.

Just like Joel was holding Phoebe. Safe, close, protected, valued. Because Joel cared about her sister, loved her. Pip darted a glance at Matt's face.

He was busy talking to Levi behind them; he'd

held her close without thinking about it. He'd just done it.

What did that mean?

Perci nudged her and Pip glanced at her twin. There was a look in Perci's eyes that told her they were going to have to talk. And fast.

MATT KNEW EXACTLY WHAT HE WAS DOING. Masterson was a small town. Rumors that he'd entered the dance with one of the Tyler sisters would hit every corner of the small community center quickly. He had no doubt they'd been seen in the parking lot, too.

Everyone would be assuming there was something between them. Exactly as he'd wanted.

He wanted everyone to know he and Pip were together. Not only for the satisfaction of knowing other men would respect that claim but for the fact that it would hopefully keep people from bombarding Pip.

He and Pip were a few feet behind Joel. The rest of their group came in behind them. Nate and Perci were sniping at each other again. Pan was laughing at something Levi had said.

It was normal, typical. It was family.

His family. Yes, there were four Tylers added in to the mix, but Matt didn't mind in the least.

In fact, he was damned proud to be with them.

Matt pulled the woman he wanted closer to his side.

26

Perci had almost missed what that ass Nate said to her.

Something about her dress being a bit too short. Of course, it was—it was Phoebe's, and they'd had to hem it up an inch or so a year ago when her sister had snagged it on something at church. It was four inches shorter on her than it was her older sister.

They didn't exactly have closets full of clothes. Especially dressy clothes. What they had, they'd shared between the four of them for years now.

Perci had actually been feeling pretty good about how she looked tonight. Tylers might not have much, but they tried to take care of what they had. Not like him. The hat on his head probably cost more than her dress and Pan's combined.

He would never understand that, though. She'd seen how he had looked around Jasper's Place. It wasn't exactly a high-class establishment. But her family liked it.

Perci told herself not to care what Nate the Great thought about any of it, but it was hard. Had the man ever struggled for anything in his life? Had any of the Mastersons? Did they have a clue what it was like to worry about where the money to feed their family was going to come from?

So many nights she and her sisters had sat in the attic, which had masqueraded as Pan's room, though it was far too small for that, worrying about where the money for food was going to come from. The last two years had been some of the hardest of her life. Things had been easier when her mother had been alive—for one thing, they hadn't had the medical bills they had now.

Things were going to get easier. Someday. Joel had already asked her what had happened the night her mother had died, and he'd promised her he'd find the answers. There had been state cops out there that night, too. Joel had already found conflicting accident reports.

The possibility for an insurance settlement had been mentioned.

Perci was afraid to hope, though. Hope was a good way to get yourself smacked in the head by life, after all.

Her eyes landed on her twin. They hadn't been in the building five minutes, and Pip already had that look on her face that said she was hitting panic mode.

Pip thought the rest of the family didn't know that she still feared practically everything to do with people. But Perci knew. How could she not? Pip was so damned scared.

Perci started to step toward her sister, to protect like she always had.

Someone else was there first.

Matt stepped up to Pip's side—he hadn't been that far away from her sister at all—and took Pip's hand in his. Separated her sister from the room, putting his big body between Pip and the crowd. Protecting her.

Pip looked up at him with an expression on her face that Perci had never seen there before.

It gave her a weird feeling in her gut. Like Pip almost didn't need Perci to protect her any longer.

She'd been protecting Pip their entire lives. The idea that some guy was there now unsettled her.

She knew it was crazy, but she'd never thought even once since they'd lost their mother and their world changed that there would possibly be a guy or two show up to unbalance their world again.

She should have. Her sisters were beautiful, wonderful, kind, loving women who deserved men to love them for exactly who they were. Phoebe had found that first, with Joel. So out of the blue, so quickly, so high stakes that everything could have been lost.

Now here was his brother, barely able to look away from Pip.

With Phoebe and Pan both out at the Masterson place now, it was just Perci and Pip at home. Doing the things that they'd always done, plus more.

If Pip and Matt got serious, what would happen next? Would her sister leave, too?

Perci could deal, though, if it meant Pip ended up as happy as Phoebe. Her family happy was all Perci really wanted in the world. Especially Pip.

She watched the two for a long time and contemplated what she had to do to help her sister be happy. The way Pip deserved. The way Pip hadn't been in a very long time.

Whether Perci wanted to accept it or not, the only choice she had was to step back and let things happen between Matt and Pip the way they happened.

27

SHE HADN'T DANCED WITH A MAN IN YEARS, but as Matt put his hot hands on her waist and pulled her closer, Pip felt her skin tighten with a mix of nerves and anticipation.

Pip wasn't stupid. She hadn't missed exactly what the people around them were thinking. They were thinking there was something between her and Matt. And they were watching to see exactly what that something was.

She could have told them all he was just a friend—becoming a good one.

She could have said he was just a family connection, thanks to her sister.

She could have told them anything at all. But

the truth was she didn't know exactly what Matt was.

Or what she wanted him to be.

He was strong and hard against her, and she could feel his heat surrounding her. And he was holding her far too close for it to be just casual.

She didn't know how she felt about that, either. Pip wanted to curl up against him, right where she was.

Pip hadn't been this confused about a man in a really, really long time.

28

IT WAS SO QUAINT. ROWLAND HONESTLY
thought he saw gingham on a few of the women.
The dance was held at the local community center, a white building probably built in the 1950s.
It was old, tacky, and filled to the brim with the
citizens of Masterson all decked out in their
finest.

There was actual lace and ruffles and a string
tie or two.

Rowland was a man on a mission.

He was finding his Gretta tonight. And he
wasn't stopping until he had Perci Tyler's agree-
ment to do exactly what he wanted her to do.
Rowland was a healthy man, and that thought

elicited more than just business plans for a long moment or two.

He'd never been with a redhead before. Or at least he couldn't remember if he had. There were a few times in his twenties when he wasn't entirely certain what he'd been with. Not times he was proud of, but ones he owned.

Personal responsibility, and all that.

He pushed his way through the crowd, looking for the handful of production assistants who trailed after him everywhere. He'd already told them to keep an eye out for a cluster of small, beautiful redheads.

Rowland had trained his people well. They'd find every redhead in the place before it was over.

Rowland didn't have to look too hard to find those redheaded women himself. It seemed almost a given that if he found one of those damned larger-than-life Masterson brothers, he'd find at least one or two of those Tylers.

Apparently tonight was going to be no exception. The first one he saw was the tallest one. The strawberry blonde who worked for the Mastersons.

He'd caught her on her hands and knees mopping the kitchen last time he'd been out there.

Hard worker, and he'd taken advantage of coming up behind her without her knowing he was there. He'd watched her a good five minutes before he'd made his presence known.

Pandora Tyler—unfortunate name there—was built just the way a man liked. That was evident tonight. The green dress she wore was simple, yet flattered every curve. Ridiculous how beautiful the girl was—she was the most classically beautiful of her sisters—it was wasted here in the back country.

And she had three older sisters nearly as beautiful who'd entered the community center right behind her. Rowland was a man, and it was damned hard not to appreciate. Even if he preferred a more sophisticated type of woman.

Phoebe Tyler Masterson looked just perfect right there next to her tall, broad-shouldered husband, and it was hard to miss. They were the darlings of the town. Rowland had certainly gotten an earful when he'd asked around.

Strangely enough, the Masterson citizens didn't know too much about the Tyler girls, but they were eager to chat about the four brothers who were such pillars of their community—the sheriff, the physician, the veterinarian, and the rancher. Tall, good-looking, successful, and strong, the Masterson brothers drew attention wherever they went.

It was almost ridiculously difficult for an ordinary man to compete in this little hamlet, where women were outnumbered almost two to one.

Someone should make a movie about them sometime. About some type of mystery they'd solved or something. It was an idea for later. He might not like the small-town life himself, but Rowland knew his audience did. And he was all about his audience—they were his paycheck, after all.

Pandora and Phoebe were beautiful, but it was the women who entered behind them who were his true objective.

Once he figured out who was who, that was.

He hadn't realized they were *that* identical. He should have. That vet had told him they were. But every time he'd seen the two, it had been Perci who'd stood out. The sister had hidden herself from him almost deliberately.

From everyone, really.

It took him a moment to study the two, but body language always told its own story. Perci was comfortable in the simple sundress she wore, and in the crowd in general.

Her twin was most definitely not. She looked afraid, to be honest. Shy, a little awkward, even. And that damned Matt Masterson was hovering over her. Protectively.

Like Masterson had before.

She worked with horses, didn't she? And her twin was a nurse.

His Gretta had been riding a horse like she'd spent hours in the saddle of the big beasts. And it hadn't been a small, dainty creature the rider had been controlling. It had looked to be a red half-wild animal far too big for a fairy to ride.

The Tyler sisters all looked like live-action Tinkerbells.

Every time he saw them he became more and more convinced his phantom Gretta was one of those Tyler sisters.

The eldest had been on her honeymoon. The youngest had hair that was just too light.

And Perci refused to say whether it was her or not. Just smiled at him every time he mentioned it. Mysteriously. Because she knew who it was.

He'd never asked the last sister, had he? Had he even spoken to her? She'd been there the day he'd stopped off at the Tyler ranch. He thought he'd said something to her then, but he just didn't remember.

Yes. The dust-covered, sweaty little female who'd been with Masterson that day. He hadn't paid much attention to her at all after Perci had returned home. He'd never gone for the tomboy type.

He hadn't thought his Gretta was one, either.

But...Perci Tyler's manner was all wrong. Even for that five-minute glimpse he'd had of his Gretta, she'd been quiet, and shy, and hurting. Vulnerable. Made a man want to protect her.

Much like Matt Masterson was hovering over the other twin.

It made him think, made him wonder if maybe he'd been an idiot, after all. Everything added up. Perci was supposed to have been at the hospital that night. Her sister was identical. Her sister worked with horses. Her sister was the quiet one. The one the others most likely wanted to protect, for some reason. The most vulnerable, apparently.

That was obvious in the way she always had a sister by her side in the crowd tonight.

And Masterson had barely taken his eyes off her.

Rowland made a point of asking for information from the next woman he danced with. She was around the same age as all the Tyler sisters and he figured she'd know quite a bit. She seemed like the type.

"I suppose everyone is talking about them again," she said, when he asked about the redheads with the Mastersons, as if he didn't know exactly who the sisters were.

There was a bite in his partner's tone that intrigued him.

"Oh?"

"They thought they were all too good for Masterson. Barely came around the town at all. Kept to themselves out at that dumpy old ranch of their father's. Until that older girl got involved with Joel. She almost got him killed."

"Oh? I'm afraid I haven't heard the story yet." To be honest, he hadn't paid much attention to the married Masterson-Tyler pair. "What happened?"

"Tom Rutherford was using a corner of the Tyler ranch to grow drugs for revenge. He hated Phoenix Tyler and the Tyler sisters. I guess he dragged Phoebe out of the cabin she was sharing with Joel at the time and nearly killed her. Would have if the twins and two of the Masterson brothers hadn't shown up. Rumor is that Matt pulled Pip and Phoebe out of a raging river. It was the talk around here for weeks a few months back."

"And Pip is? I'm afraid I can't tell them all apart."

"It's no wonder. They all look alike and have those silly names. Pip is that one, in the light-green shirt, denim skirt. She works the ranch with her father, I think. I never even knew Perci had sisters until a few months ago. They keep to themselves. Well, they did. Until Phoebe took Joel. Now they're all over the Mastersons. Heard Levi told some of his friends to stay away from Pandora, too." There was a bitter light of jealousy in his dance partner's eyes. Rowland had never found that attractive in a woman. He felt for the younger Tyler in that moment.

Raymond had never been able to resist poking the bear. "And which one is Pandora?"

"That one. With the reddish-blond hair. Levi's right next to her. Hasn't left her side all night, damn it. Or danced with anyone other than her or her sisters. He never used to be like that. He's wearing that blue shirt."

Rowland dutifully looked toward the Mastersons. Levi Masterson was right there with his three brothers, the beautiful Pandora next to him. "So they are involved then? What about the twins? I take it they're here with the other Masterson brothers?"

The woman, he couldn't remember her name, almost snarled. "Not that I know of. But you can't see a Masterson brother around this town without seeing one of them anymore. Perci and Nate, though, rumor has it they despise each other. Work together at the hospital and are always fighting. Levi has that Pan with him all the time. Some say she's his housekeeper, but I think she's just using that."

"And the other one? Pip? She's the twin in green?"

"Hmm. No one knows much about her. Just that she's a Tyler. I think it's because her sisters keep her quiet for some reason. Likely there's something wrong with her. Mentally. It's the only thing that makes sense."

Catty women had always disgusted him. This one, though she was reasonably pretty and her father an important man in the town, was no exception.

Rowland looked over his partner's shoulder.

There certainly didn't seem to be anything wrong with Pip Tyler. She was standing between two of the Masterson brothers, looking more and more like his Gretta by the minute.

Rowland was a writer, first and foremost. Obsessed with the story. The characters. In that moment, he just knew. Pip Tyler was his Gretta—not Perci.

As she took the dance floor with Matt Masterson, something else clicked in his brain. Keith, Gretta's brother's best friend, was a tall, dark-haired man much like the Masterson brothers. His storyline was still in flux. Rowland hadn't known what to do with him, how to resolve it, but he'd wanted to give the guy a happy ending. His audience would be expecting it.

Rowland just hadn't known how.

Until this very moment, watching the vet take the girl who would be his Gretta into his arms.

He didn't just want Pip, did he?

How was he going to convince a man like Matt Masterson to be in his next film?

Rowland hadn't exactly made friends with the man. Still, he'd always enjoyed a challenge.

ROWLAND WANTED HER TO LOOK AT HIM. That's why he'd crossed the room and asked what he had.

Pip Tyler just looked up at him out of those seriously enchanting blue eyes, like she hadn't quite heard him correctly. "Excuse me?"

"I said, may I have this dance, please?" He held out his left hand to her and tried his most charming smile.

She hesitated, looked around the room shyly. Just like Gretta would have—if she'd been real, that was. He so wanted this woman to help him make Gretta real. He needed her. But how to make her see?

"I'm not Perci."

"I know. Pip, I believe. I don't want to dance with Perci. I want to dance with you." Rowland had taken the first opportunity he had. The instant Matt Masterson stepped away from her, he'd swooped in.

He couldn't lose his Gretta to some cowboy. No matter how much he wanted Matt for Keith. He needed to secure her as his Gretta first.

She did look damned good next to the vet, though. With the proper costuming, she and Masterson would look perfect on the screen together.

"But why? I know what you want from my sister." The wariness made him doubly careful, but Rowland was determined. He wanted five damned minutes away from everyone else to just talk to this girl. Figure her out. He was an excellent judge of character, after all. Character was his stock in trade. And Rowland prided himself on being good at what he did. "She's not interested."

"Oh? I believe I can make it worth her while." And there was always a way to get what he wanted. Usually with cold, hard cash. Everyone in town had loved to talk about the Tylers, after all. Rumor had it they were strapped for cash. Extremely so.

Everyone could be bought. Even if he had to use the rest of the Tylers as extras—everyone could be bought. He just suspected the Tylers had an actual cold, hard cash price. He just had to find it.

He didn't doubt his Gretta was no exception. But what was this small woman's ultimate price?

"Dance with me." Rowland took a gamble—he wrapped his hand around her much smaller one, took the soda out of her other hand and sat it on the table next to her, and guided her onto the dance floor before she even had a chance to protest.

Rowland didn't miss Masterson's glower from clear across the room at the refreshment table. Score! He'd nabbed Masterson's girl. Rowland smiled back at the man.

Then he looked back at that girl.

She trembled against him, and for a moment he thought it was because she found him attractive. Then he looked closer.

Pip was frightened of him. Of course, she would be. It fit her character, didn't it? "I'm not an ax murderer, and I don't harm kittens or horses. In fact, both kind of scare me—more than an ax murderer, actually. I'm Rowland, by the way. You're Pip. I watched you the other day, with Dr. Masterson, and that yellow horse."

"Wind Lover. She's a buckskin, not yellow," she said quietly. "Welcome to Masterson, Mr. Bowles."

"Thank you. I've been here for about a week now. I'm looking for a few places to shoot a movie. Someone mentioned I might want to take a look at your place. I am going to use the Masterson place. If I can get the brothers to agree. Apparently, it's hard to get the four of them to agree on anything."

She smiled softly. Rowland blinked. She had a killer smile, this girl. Perfect white teeth, soft pink kissable lips slightly tilted at one end. She'd look beautiful on the screen. Even more beautiful in some lucky man's bed. He strongly suspected she'd already been in Masterson's. Why else would the guy be glaring at Rowland so hard? He threatened Matt Masterson, didn't he? Rowland tried not to smirk.

"They know their own minds, don't they?"

"Rather like you Tylers, from what I'm hearing." Rowland wanted to hold her closer, but he didn't dare push her.

Pip Tyler was the very definition of skittish. A wave of something completely foreign rushed through him—an almost desire to protect this lost little waif. Strange. It had to be because she was part fairy, or something. Able to make a man forget his own head somehow.

That was what it had to be.

Pip Tyler was going to enchant every male viewer his film had. Rowland was counting on that.

29

Pip forced herself not to panic. It was just dancing. And the guy holding her wasn't some scary drunk.

It wasn't like dancing with Matt. The men were close to the same size; Matt was a little bigger, a little tougher. A little stronger.

This man's hands didn't burn her through her clothes, like Matt's had. She wasn't intensely aware of how he was breathing against her.

No, all she could think about was ending the dance and putting space between them. He hadn't done anything to threaten her. His hands weren't too tight, he wasn't brushing too close against her, and there was plenty of room between them.

But he wasn't Matt.

Dancing with Matt had been entirely different. She'd actually enjoyed that. Had wanted to cuddle up against that broad chest and just let the music float around them.

She knew that was ridiculous.

He had held her hand. Ask her specifically to ride with him. Sat next to her at Jasper's. It had been her that he had danced with, no one else. He'd ask for the first dance, and she'd given it to him. But at least three other dances had played since then. And until five minutes ago, Matt hadn't left her side once. What did that mean? Or did it mean anything at all?

She was so consumed with thoughts of Matt that she missed what the man holding her had asked. "Excuse me?"

"I said, would you like to have dinner with me tomorrow evening?"

Pip almost stumbled in the dance. She looked into the man's brown eyes.

He meant it.

Why? Did he think by going through her he could convince Perci to do whatever it was he wanted? He wouldn't be the first man to try. Or even the second. Or third.

No, the third man to try that had been Jay Gunderson, hadn't it? That had a chill running down her back. Pip forced herself to remain calm.

"Why?" Honesty and directness was the Tyler way. Better than wasting someone's time. "What do you want from me?"

"Besides an evening with a beautiful woman?"

Now she knew he wanted something from her. There was a woman who looked just like her walking around not that far away. One who'd had his attention first.

This man wanted something. From her.

Did he think she was the easiest mark, or something? She was tired of people thinking that. "I don't like to be charmed or manipulated, Mr. Bowles. None of us Tylers do. You'll find there's a lot of Tylers in this county. And we talk."

"I'm not lying. You have to know that you're beautiful. And there's something about your eyes that are very intriguing." He smiled, an expression that had no doubt won him tons of feminine attention in Hollywood, or wherever else it was he came from. "Have you ever considered being an actress?"

"No. I haven't. I'm a rancher, Mr. Bowles.

That's the only thing I've ever considered. Why do you ask?"

"What if I told you I have a character in my upcoming film that you would be perfect for?"

"I'd tell you I thought you were crazy." She didn't know where the confidence was coming from, but she wasn't going to take any of this man's lines. She knew that was exactly what he was doing—feeding her lines. "I've been in one play my entire life. I'm not interested in repeating that experience for millions of people to watch."

The dance started to end, and she pulled away. Pip immediately looked for Matt and found him clear across the room. How had they ended up there?

Rowland Bowles was good, very good. But there was a tall, dark-haired, blue-eyed man watching her. Waiting for her.

It was Matt who Pip wanted to be with.

And not just because of safety.

But because of him. He drew her, didn't he? It was why she always looked for him when with the Mastersons. Why hadn't she realized that before?

As she stepped away from Bowles, Matt stepped toward her. And kept coming.

Was he rescuing her? Protecting her for some

reason? Had his brother asked him to? She had no doubt that Phoebe had told Joel what had happened to her years ago. They had certainly discussed the former sheriff, Clive Gunderson. Maybe that was it; maybe Joel had asked Matt to keep an eye on her tonight?

Like a babysitter.

Pip was tired of being the vulnerable one. Wasn't it time that she learned to take care of herself, even in a crowd? Normal women, twenty-three-year-old women, did not cower because of one bad experience.

She was a Tyler, and Tylers just dealt. It was time she learned to deal.

Pip stepped away from Bowles and turned from the man intent on rescuing her. It was time she made a decision for herself. To do that, she needed time to think.

30

JAY'S DADDY HADN'T WANTED HIM TO COME TO the dance tonight. Jay knew the truth; the old man was ashamed of him. Blamed him for the loss of his position as county sheriff.

Hell, it probably had been Jay's fault. Time he owned his actions, wasn't it? Jay had learned a lot in prison about what he wanted out of life.

What sheriff needed his own son arrested for running drugs through the county? His father, and his older brother Clint—who was with the Wyoming Highway Patrol—had made that clear to him. He was the family screwup and always had been.

Jay had done his time. And gotten himself clean—mostly—in prison.

Pip had helped with that. Whenever he'd been aching for something more in prison, he'd curled up in his bunk and imagined her. What he would do to her once he had her in his arms. What she would do to him.

Sweet little Pip Tyler had gotten him through some seriously dark nights. She had a naughty streak once the lights went out. Jay had taught her exactly what he wanted—in his dreams.

This building was where he had first seen her, had first discovered the woman who was meant to be his. His future, his life.

His, and no one else's.

He didn't know if she would be here tonight, but he had to try, didn't he? He'd hooked up a few months ago with Chuck and Dale—some of his buddies from pre-prison time—they'd given him a lift tonight. He'd taken advantage of it, even though the two of them were still stuck mentally in high school.

They'd never grow up, never figure things out for themselves—not like he had. Jay had plans, strong plans, for his life now.

After his father had lost the election, he retired from the Masterson County police force to work the small ranch that had been in their family for generations. While not a big place, it was certainly prosperous enough to support Jay and his old man adequately.

It would even support Jay's wife and family when the time came. If the time ever came; once he'd found the woman he wanted. He'd envied the men on his cellblock who had wives and girlfriends to come see them, to give a shit what happened to them. He'd ached for a woman of his own during those four years.

His old man had visited once in four years.

Clint hadn't visited at all.

If Jay hadn't frightened Pip so badly, she would have visited him to. He just knew that. If he hadn't been such an ass, had taken his time to get to know her, court her, even.

That had been his biggest mistake, rushing her.

She'd been so innocent; he'd terrified her.

Jay stepped inside the community center. And looked around.

31

"You shouldn't be out here alone, honey."

Pip knew immediately who was behind her, who the soft voice belonged to. She'd known he would follow. And he had. She tightened her arms around her middle and looked up at him, straight on.

No more cowering with Matt. Period. And whatever it was the man wanted from her, she was going to meet him on equal footing. And that meant honesty. "I can't breathe in there."

"I know." He didn't crowd her, and Pip appreciated that. But she wanted to be closer to him.

Pip pulled in a deep breath and stepped into his path.

"I didn't go outside, I'm still in the building."

"You hate this place, don't you?" He stepped closer. Pip fought the urge to back away. This was just Matt. Matt, who would never hurt her. Yet she still felt like a damned coward. Like a rabbit frightened of a declawed house cat.

Not that Matt was all that tame. No, he looked big and strong and...beautiful. Real. Whole.

She felt like such a fraud. A fraud who had been afraid of her own shadow for four years. When was she ever going to stop being such a coward? "Yes! Yes, I hate this place."

"Was it here that it happened?" He kept coming closer.

Pip wrapped a hand around her jumping stomach and just looked at him. She nodded quietly. "Yes. It was just like tonight. I just wanted to go outside to breathe. There were too many people. The smells, the sight, the press of people all around me. I had to come out here again. To see if I just could."

It was the first she'd spoken of this to anyone.

Her family knew what had happened, of course. Her father had wanted her to go for counseling, to get help of some kind, but Pip had refused. They hadn't been able to pay for it then, and they definitely couldn't now.

She'd been too afraid. Always, always afraid. Why?

"I didn't realize he had followed me. He grabbed me from behind. Right over there. I'd already told him I didn't want to dance. Perci had turned him down, too. And he really wanted Perci. I was his second choice, and he told me that. Said one of us was as good as the other."

A warm hand brushed the tear from her cheek. She hadn't realized she was crying. Pip firmed her voice and continued, needing to tell him what had shaped her. Maybe by putting it into words now, she could finally start to deal.

Pip just wanted to deal.

"He backed me up against the wall of the building. Then we were outside somehow. He ripped my dress, and he had his arm against my throat. I couldn't breathe. I don't think I've really breathed since that night. Since Perci came running, terrified. She said...she said she just knew I needed her. Knew where I was, even. Phoebe hit him, knocked him off me. Pan kicked him when he tried to stand up. Hard. Perci wrapped her arms around me—helped me fix my dress—and Phoebe and Pan made him go away. And then his father came. That's when it got so much worse."

32

THE FIRST REDHEADED WOMAN JAY SAW WAS wearing a light-blue dress and was damned beautiful. Made a man drool just looking at her.

For a moment he just stared, wondering. And then she turned when someone called her name, and he knew. It wasn't her.

It was the bitch twin.

She was standing next to one of her sisters; this one was slightly taller and paler. He didn't have a clue what her name was. But she'd been there that night. Had kicked his balls into his ears.

He had a score to settle with her, too. Both of them. And the eldest. The one married to that asshole Joel Masterson.

Hell, he had a score to settle with all the Tyler sisters.

Except his Pip. He'd have to get her settled, first. Then he'd deal with the sisters.

He should not have scared her like he had. Pip was the quiet one, after all. The sweet one. The one made for some man to pamper and take care of.

And that was exactly what Jay was going to do.

He'd get started tonight. Because where there was one Tyler sister, there were three more somewhere.

Pip was here, and he was going to find her.

33

IF ONE OF THOSE DAMNED GUNDERSONS HAD been within reach, Matt would just tear the sonofabitch's throat out for the way Pip looked in that moment. What was he supposed to say to her? He didn't have a clue. "I'm sorry that happened to you, baby. It wasn't right, and if I could go back in time and be here to help you that night, I would. In a heartbeat."

She looked up at him out of those blue eyes of hers, and everything in him just melted. Matt wanted to take on the world and every damned Gunderson or Rutherford or any other threat that she'd faced in the last four years.

Anything to erase the lingering fear that ate at her.

"I...never told anyone other than my sisters. My mother and father. My dad was so angry. I've never seen him so angry, or so sad. Perci still blames herself for making Jay angry. She thinks she could have turned him down easier or something. But he was so drunk. Phoebe went crazy protective, much worse than she used to be. Pan was seventeen, and he scared her, too. He hit her after she kicked him. Slapped her hard enough for her to have a black eye the next morning. I don't think she's ever been alone with a man since that night, Matt. I don't know if she's ever even been kissed."

"That's not your fault."

"Isn't it? I went outside alone. I should have told Phoebe or Perci or Pan. My father. Anyone. Instead, I just snuck away, afraid of people." Bitterness entered her words. "I've always been afraid of people, Matt. Even before. You and your brothers terrify me. What does that say about me?"

Matt didn't think, didn't plan it. He just acted. He wrapped his hands around her small waist and lifted her, until blue eyes met green. "It says that you're shy, not afraid. What is so wrong with that, honey? I think you're just fine exactly the way you are."

"Am I? Then why am I so afraid all the time? I don't want to be a coward anymore." Her whispered confession went straight through him. "I'm finished being a coward. But I just don't know how to stop."

"A coward is the last thing you are. I know. I saw it for myself, remember? No coward braves a raging flood to save her sister, honey. No coward does that."

He felt the trembling. Felt the fear in her. Fear of him?

Damn it all, the last thing Matt ever wanted was for this strong, brave, loyal, wonderful woman to ever fear him.

He lowered her slowly to the tiled floor until she was looking up at him instead of straight at him. Until her chest was pressed to his and he could smell the sweet scent of Pip. "Pip?"

"Kiss me."

Matt was sure he hadn't heard right. "Honey?"

Red hit her cheeks. "I'm sorry. I mean...will you kiss me? Just once? I've not been kissed since that night...and I...don't want to be so afraid. Not of you...I don't want to be afraid of you anymore, Matt. Not you. Not like this." Matt said a short, quiet prayer. For strength.

She pulled against his hands, her embarrassment clear. "I'm sorry. I never..."

Matt couldn't take the pain she felt in that moment. He still had his hands on her waist, and he lifted. Until her mouth was aligned with his own. "Philippa Tyler, I very much want to kiss you. And have for a very, very long time."

She stopped rambling. "Oh."

"Yes. Oh." Matt brushed those sweet lips with his own.

34

SHE'D NEVER DEMANDED A MAN KISS HER before, either. Pip had never thought she'd die from embarrassment before. But it was Matt. She didn't think he'd tell anyone.

He didn't feel like he was kissing her out of obligation.

Or to spare her feelings.

Matt wasn't rushing her, either.

Pip didn't think she could handle it if he rushed her. Instead, she just let him hold her there, off her feet, while he pressed his lips to hers.

It didn't hurt.

She wasn't having a massive panic attack at the feel of a man's hands on her.

His hands hadn't left her waist, just held her strong and tight against him. Steady.

Safe. She felt safe kissing this man. And that meant all the world to her.

This time the tears that leaked out were tears of joy.

He started to pull away. Pip wrapped her fingers in the cotton of his shirt and just held him tighter.

For the first time since she was nineteen, Pip kissed a man right back.

35

Rowland had never let a few things like propriety and public appearances keep him from getting what he wanted. He'd watched Pip hurry off the dance floor, and he'd started after her. If he could catch her before Masterson did, all the better. He'd always liked a bit of competition in life. It got a man's blood pumping, after all.

It didn't happen. Jenny, one of his newest assistants, caught him near the door to the hall. "Mr. Bowles, Andrew said you wanted to see me."

He hadn't. He'd only brought the girl last minute when another had had to back out. He'd had the spot on payroll, so this girl had gotten it. Andrew was messing with the girl, probably just out of spite. Rowland started to tell her off to get her to leave him alone but thought better of it when he looked at her a bit more closely.

He might have a better use for her.

She wasn't any older than Pip Tyler, and barely much bigger. Her hair was a light strawberry blond, and she was a very pretty woman. When a man looked closer. When the man looked beyond the wholesome nerdy goody-goodness of her.

She was the type most in Hollywood ate for lunch. He'd eaten quite a few just like her himself. Back in the day of him not being a good person and all. He'd only brought her on this trip because she was a native of a small town just like Masterson. She knew how places like this worked, didn't she? And that was what he'd needed. Just in case.

Hell, she'd probably grown up with two dozen women exactly like the Tyler sisters. And he could use that. But what was her name again? Fortunately, his memory served him well. "Jen, I did. Would you like to dance? We need to talk. There's something I need you to do for me."

"Of course, sir. Whatever you need."

Jenny needed to be careful making that kind of offer in their profession. There were far too many who would take the girl up on that. In ways he doubted this pretty little ingénue understood. Hell, half the men he considered his best friends would devour her at the first opportunity they got.

Innocence wasn't often found in Hollywood, after all. Jenny would become a tasty treat for some bastard somewhere. It was just a matter of time.

He took Jenny's hand in his and led her out to the dance floor. For a few moments, they just danced while he got his thoughts in order. While she just stared up at him, a puzzled expression in her light-green eyes. Very pretty eyes that she hid behind tinted glasses. Why did she do that?

"Sir?"

"Jenny, sweetie, call me Rowland." *Sir* made him feel like an idiot. "I need you to do something for me. You see those women over there, the trio of redheads? Small, beautiful redheads, *just* like you? You'll fit in perfectly over there, won't you?"

"Yes. I suppose."

"Their sister Pip—she's in the restroom now, I think—is perfect for our Gretta. Yet she doesn't want to be. We need to convince her. I need you to learn everything you can about the Tylers of Masterson County. Help me find a way to convince her to do exactly what we need. No matter what you have to do, understand?"

"Yes, sir. I'll do my best."

"That's all I can ask." Rowland remained silent for the rest of the dance, though he wanted to ask the girl in his arms a million questions about why she did the things she did. Probe to the bottom of her character, like he wanted to everyone. He had a lot to think about, and he didn't need to get distracted by the press of his nerdy little assistant's skinny body in his arms, the brush of smallish breasts against his chest, or the sweet scent of her perfume. Or how pink her lips looked. How he wished he could be the man to ultimately devour this sweet little innocent in his arms. He was such a pervert at times.

Rowland ruthlessly forced thoughts of his assistant out of his head.

He had work to do. And that was all that mattered.

36

————

It took Jay a while to find her. The crowd was starting to thicken. Push against him. Some people just wanted to stare. Gossip and whisper. Damned inbred fools. They'd made his life miserable from the time he been a teenager. They probably wouldn't stop.

He finally found her. Wrapped up in some damned Masterson's arms. The same one who'd been with her at the diner that day.

Next to her. Touching her.

Rage boiled. Jay wanted to explode, to rip the damned community center to shreds. Destroy them all for even looking at her in her green blouse and modest denim skirt. His Pip didn't need to flash her assets to be beautiful, did she?

Joel Masterson had taken four years of his life from him; this Masterson was not taking his future from him. Pip was his. There wasn't anything he wouldn't do to get her.

Masterson's hands were all over her. Pip was letting him do it. Why was she letting him? Just how involved were they?

Had she slept with him?

A man like Masterson wouldn't be content with just kissing and petting for long. Not with a woman like Pip. No, Masterson wanted to screw Pip; Jay had no doubt about that.

Most of the men who'd watched her tonight probably had that same thought. Damn them all.

Pip was his.

Jay just stood in the corner and watched her for the longest time. That damned Masterson finally left her side, headed toward the men's room. Jay fantasized for a quick moment about slipping into the restroom behind the man and shoving a blade into Masterson's ribs. Teaching him a lesson once and for all.

Pip was his—his.

No damned Masterson was going to take her away.

He thought about asking her to dance himself. Then thought about it again; he'd scared her so badly that first night they'd met. He didn't want to frighten her even more. Especially in front of the whole damned town.

His daddy had made that clear, after that night. Had told him that Pip Tyler was just a young, innocent girl, and he should have known better than to try what he had so publicly. Should've stuck to the more experienced bitches out there. Women closer to Jay's own age. His daddy had said that all he had done was make trouble for his father. And scare that girl. Badly.

His daddy had had to go out to their place and threaten the sisters to keep them quiet, to keep Jay out of jail on an attempted-rape charge, of all things. Said that he'd scared them right good. That they wouldn't talk. For anything.

His father could be damned terrifying when he wanted to be. Jay had the scars on his back to prove it. He could only imagine what it had been like for Pip to face his daddy that night.

She had been so young, so small. Damn it. His father shouldn't have done that to her. And he doubted his father had stopped that night. His daddy would have enjoyed having the Tyler sisters frightened of him. Would have got off on that power.

What else had his daddy done to Pip that Jay did not know about?

No, he was better off waiting, planning just exactly how to get to her. Still, it had hurt him to watch her dance with that damned movie director everyone was fawning over, then take off down the hall with Masterson on her heels.

It hurt him.

She should be wrapped up in his arms, not some other man's.

He'd waited in literal hell for four years to have the woman who was meant to be his. He'd survived by imagining how sweet their life together was going to be, how she'd smile just at him when he'd come in from working the ranch. How she'd hold his sons close some day. He'd even half imagined a redheaded daughter or two, just because women liked daughters. Little girls that looked like their mother would be just fine with him.

Jay was going to give that woman everything she could possibly want. Make her see that she didn't need that family of hers, that she would have him. He'd give her enough kids to replace those sisters and brothers of hers in her heart. And even his daddy and brother Clint. Clint's wife already had a baby on the way.

There'd be plenty of family for Pip when she was with him.

If his father hadn't terrified her so badly she didn't want anything to do with her future father-in-law.

Which was a possibility. Jay remembered his father's particular brand of terrorism well, after all. Jay had gotten off light. It had been *Clint* who'd borne the worst of their daddy's teachings.

No. It would probably be best if he took Pip back to the ranch he'd inherited from his mother's father ten years ago. It was all his and his father had nothing to do with it. It wasn't successful yet, but Jay was willing to make it be. It was a bit rundown at the moment, but that would give him something to do while he planned how to get his girl. He'd make it a home.

For her.

It would be her home; she could decorate it exactly how she wanted. And he'd even get her a puppy to love.

Anything that woman wanted, he'd get it.

Somehow. For her.

He would have her soon, he would just have to be patient.

In the meantime, he needed to plan on how he was going to get her away from those sisters of hers. Forever.

That was what he was going to have to do— he'd just take her to his place and keep her away from their families. Build a new family for the both of them. Just the two of them and their four or five children, forever.

37

An hour into the dance, and Perci was ready to go home. She used to enjoy events like this until Jay Gunderson had attacked her sister.

Now it was just tedious. If Phoebe hadn't needed her there, Perci would have just stayed home with the boys and some popcorn. She'd rather watch Disney than deal with the idiot flirtations the men of Masterson County were pushing in her direction.

She had some fun talking with her cousins Nicole, Maggie, Augie, Junie, and Em, and watching Pip be pursued by Matt. Perci was grateful for the time with her family, who were also her friends.

But Pip was the one who would always worry her the most.

Matt caused her quite a bit of concern. The last thing on earth she ever wanted was for Pip to get hurt. Of all her sisters, Pip was her world, her absolute world. If something would happen to her again...well, Perci just couldn't think about that.

Not that she thought Matt would hurt her sister. Matt was a good man; all the Mastersons were, even that prick Nate. It was just with Perci that he was a real jerk. Nate had been wonderful, almost kind, with her sisters.

Pip being pursued by Matt was going to change things again. For all of them. Even Perci. She was mulling over one of those small problems when she finally caught up with Phoebe and Pan near the refreshments—after a particularly annoying question from a rancher who'd been on the make and pissed she'd turned down his offer to go out back to his truck for a beer.

"If one more person asks me which Masterson brother I belong to, I'm going to scream," she said to her sisters.

"I know exactly what you're feeling," Pan said. She practically growled the words, and Perci looked at her. Pan sighed before continuing. "Apparently Levi has told several of his friends that I'm off the market. And to keep their hands to themselves. Not that I want their hands on me, but I would like to at least have the choice myself. The jerk. I don't know what he was thinking. I don't need him to play big brother. I'm perfectly capable of deciding who to date or not. If I want to even date at all. But he's got this weird idea that I need him to protect me from every penis in Masterson County."

Perci snickered. She didn't think it was *big brother* that Levi wanted to play with Pan. Far from it. More like *Naked Wrestling.*

Of all of her sisters, Pan was the most innocent, naive. Even Pip wasn't a virgin, like Pan. The youngest sister hadn't even been kissed. She had no clue about how men actually were.

Living with the Masterson brothers probably wasn't helping—they weren't exactly normal men, after all.

If Levi Masterson was sending out those type of clues, Pandora would totally miss it. Perci's eyes met Phoebe's, and they shared silent laughter.

Still, what was Levi Masterson planning for her sister? And what did that mean for the rest of them?

Phoebe and Joel, Pip and Matt, Pan and Levi, they were all pairing off and quickly—was it any wonder people were assuming she and Nate had arrived together? That they were a done deal or something?

No, it wasn't. Damn it.

And it wasn't going to happen.

Perci distracted herself by studying the crowd; looking for her twin, as always. She'd kept one eye open and on Pip from the moment they'd been born.

And there Pip was on the dance floor, wrapped up in Matt's arms. Again.

A hell of a lot closer than they had been the first time they had danced. As if something had shifted between them, deepened.

Oh hell, things were about to change for the Tylers again, weren't they?

38

PIP WAS SCREWING AROUND WITH THAT VET. Jay had no doubt about it. That Masterson had gotten to his girl. He had taken her from him. Somehow Jay had lost her.

His Pip.

Fury unlike any other threatened to drown him. To burn him completely. She had no business wrapped up in that Masterson's arms like that. Those damned Mastersons ruined everything, took everything, away from his family.

Jay tried to bite back the anger and fury consuming him. But he couldn't do it. He needed an outlet. Before he did something he completely regretted.

Jay stepped outside, lit a cigarette, and just waited. Thought. Planned.

A trio of young guys walked by him. He recognized one of them.

Her brother. Tall, skinny, and cocky. He acted like he owned the world. He'd been there that night four years ago, but he had just been a damned kid. Jay hadn't paid him any attention.

That was going to change tonight.

"Hey, Tyler, saw those sisters of yours inside. Looking just as hot as they used to. Nice to see some things don't change while a man's in prison. Had quite a few enjoyable nights thinking of those twins in my bunk with me."

Phoenix Tyler stopped walking. Stared at him a minute as if he was trying to place him. The kid's mouth pulled up in a snarl. "Gunderson. Let me guess, out on good behavior? Or did Daddy talk to the parole board? How much did he pay them to let you out?"

The boy stepped closer. Jay had to hand it to him. Most guys around here were afraid of him and stepped back instead of forward.

"You go anywhere near one of my sisters, and I'll show you how my daddy taught me to fish. Using your own insides. Understand me? You'll never get near my sisters again. Ever. Your daddy's not the sheriff to threaten people into keeping quiet anymore. Keep that in mind. The sheriff's on our side now."

Jay just smirked. He wanted to pound the shit out of the kid, but the boy had a point. If Jay laid a finger on him, it would be back to prison. Then this kid would win.

Masterson would win.

He'd have all that time with Pip that Jay wouldn't. And Jay would lose Pip forever. The time would come when he could take care of the rest of the Tylers one by one, if needed. But it wasn't now.

"Tyler, you'll give my best to little Pip, won't you? I saw her inside. She's looking mighty good, better than Perci could ever hope to. Makes a man just want to flip that skirt of hers right up and see what's beneath. She still favor pink panties?"

That was exactly what he needed to say. Phoenix Tyler swung, his fist connecting with Jay's face.

Jay attacked.

Unfortunately for him, he'd forgotten Phoenix Tyler hadn't come to the dance alone.

Two Tyler cousins jumped right in. Jay went to the ground.

39

Rowland watched everything that happened with mild curiosity; people watching was his favorite pastime, after all. It was a great way to get fodder for the movies.

He watched the older man provoke the boy, and he watched the boy and his friends rise to the bait. Why had the guy done that?

There was more there going on. Rowland was half tempted to figure it out. But he had other things to do.

Pip was inside. He wanted to dance with her at least one more time without Masterson getting in his way.

The doors opened, and two men stepped out.

Mastersons.

Of course. It was always Mastersons in this county, wasn't it?

The sheriff pulled the young guy off the older man. "Back off, Phoenix. Before I have to take you in. Probation, remember?" The boy's nose was bleeding, but he'd given better than he'd gotten. Of course, that could have been because of the two young guys who had helped him.

Rowland just watched.

Sheriff Masterson reached down and pulled the older man to his feet. "Gunderson. I should've known. Phoenix, what happened?"

The second Masterson brother stayed silent, just crossed his arms over his massive chest; he was the big one, then. The physician. Rowland didn't remember his name. Something biblical. All the Masterson brothers had biblical names.

Rowland just stayed where he was and observed.

"He said something about my sisters. About Pip. About her underwear, Joel. He's never to look at her again. He's never going to hurt her again. If he does, I will kill him myself."

The mention of the woman Rowland wanted had his attention sharpening.

The sheriff smacked the boy upside the head. Rowland got it now. The kid was a Tyler, making him family to the sheriff. Pip's brother? The resemblance was certainly there, though the lights of the parking lot were not the greatest.

"Watch what you say, Phoenix; words have power, too. I'd hate for you to get into more trouble because of a damned Gunderson. You leave this guy to me. He won't be getting near Pip ever again. I can promise you that. Your sisters are inside. You might get in there. Warn Perci and the others that some trash has blown through the parking lot. Tell my brother Matt especially, understand? Make it clear to him that Jay Gunderson's back around."

"Why?" the boy asked. Apparently, he wasn't the brightest of the Tylers. Rowland had certainly known what the sheriff had been getting at.

"Just do it," the sheriff said. "Pip came with him tonight, understand me? And he takes anything to do with Pip very, very seriously."

That's the way it was. Rowland had just gotten his suspicions confirmed. Before he was going to get to his Gretta, he was going to have to get to Matt Masterson first.

How the hell was he supposed to do that?

40

THE REST OF THE DANCE WAS PRACTICALLY idyllic in Pip's experience—until Phoenix came rushing in. It was obvious he had been fighting with someone, and Pip felt trepidation run through her. Phoenix was a magnet for trouble, and she understood why. That didn't make it any easier for them to deal with.

Since Phoebe had hooked up with Joel, Phoenix had been a bit more manageable. It wasn't her he was looking for; it was Matt.

"Masterson, your brother told me to tell you that Gunderson's back. He's here tonight."

Cold went straight through her. Pip's hands tightened on Matt's arms where he held her. She fought to keep the tremors from tearing her apart. She'd finally found her resolve to put Jay Gunderson behind her and get on with living a real life without the fear.

The only reason she had been able to come tonight was with the understanding that Jay Gunderson avoided town gathers. That he wouldn't be there tonight.

That his father and brother most likely wouldn't be there tonight, either. Clint, Jay's older brother, hadn't been seen much in the past year or so. She'd never had a problem with the older Gunderson brother—not many people did. He wasn't like his father.

Clive Gunderson made a point of glaring at her every time she walked by him in town, reminding her of everything he'd threatened that day.

Pip fought to hold onto her composure, to not let the world around her see the fear. It seemed like she'd been fighting that same battle for more than four years now.

Suddenly it wasn't her brother in her view; it was the man holding her. Matt scooped her off her feet and held her pressed against his chest. Her fingers tightened on the cotton of his shirt. "You're okay, baby. He's never going to hurt you again. I promise that. No matter what I have to do, he'll never come near you again."

"I want to go home, Matt. I'm done. I don't want to be here any longer."

"Then we go, right now. We just need to tell your sisters we're going. And I'll take you home. Is your dad there?"

She shook her head. "No, Dad's still down in Texas at the W-Deane ranch. He and the owner are working on an experimental organic beef program. Dad won't be home for a few more weeks. He's delayed because of some trouble the owner had. The boys are staying with my uncle this evening."

"So your house is empty?"

"Yes." Suddenly she didn't want to go back to an empty house. To be alone with just her memories. Her stupid fears. If she did, she'd just lose what resolve she'd found.

Matt seemed to understand that. "Then we'll head back to my place until Pan and Phoebe can join us. And we'll just forget Jay Gunderson even exists. How does that sound?"

Like she was being a big wimp, needing the big handsome strong man to rescue her.

She wasn't certain how she felt about that, but he didn't give her any time to protest. Nor did he let go of her, even once. And as they crossed the crowded community center, the only thing Pip could focus on was the feel of his strong, hot hand wrapped around hers.

41

Matt could easily sense her confusion, and it made him furious. That son of a bitch was no longer going to have the power to hurt her. No matter what he had to do. He'd gotten the rest of the details from his brother when he'd stopped to explain to Joel where he was taking Pip. He'd seen the fury in his older brother's eyes, too.

Joel had had to deal with Gunderson tonight. Gunderson was very fortunate that Matt hadn't been there; if he had, he probably would've decked the guy for what he had done to Pip.

Instead, Matt just focused on her.

She didn't say anything other than a quiet thank you until he had her back at his house. Until they were digging into some of the homemade ice cream Pan had left in the freezer. "It's Pan's recipe, isn't it? She's always made the best ice cream."

Matt nodded. One thing he could say about his housekeeper: the woman knew her way around the kitchen. He was just glad there'd been some ice cream left. Especially as he watched Pip lick it off the spoon like a dainty little kitten. "I think I've put on ten pounds since Pan took the job."

"I think I've lost it. I can cook, but Pan always makes the best desserts. Thank you, for tonight. Sorry to cut your evening short because of me."

"Pip, you are my evening. The only reason I went to the damned dance at all was because you were going. I'm not going to lie to you about that."

"I..."

He could easily see the confusion in her big blue eyes; now wasn't the time for any serious discussions about what he wanted from her.

But he couldn't resist touching her, just once. She'd left her hair down, soft and silky around her shoulders. Matt brushed it gently. Ran one finger over her cheek.

The sunburn was still there, but it didn't detract from how soft the woman's skin was. Her lower lip trembled.

"It's you I want to be with. No one else. Whether that's in that damned community center or right here on my couch. It's you."

42

PIP COULDN'T BREATHE. THIS MAN MEANT it. "I—"

"I know I confuse you and I didn't mean to blindside you, honey. But I'm not going to lie or hide it from you. I want honesty between us. If you want me to scoot back over here, then I'll do it."

She didn't. That was the last thing she wanted. Pip wanted the exact opposite.

Pip reached out and brushed a hand across his cheek. "Matt..."

She looked at him for a moment, a long moment, until she finally figured out just who the man in front of her was. Figured out what he wanted from her. "I don't want you to move over there. I don't know exactly what it is I do want yet, but I don't want you over there."

His indrawn breath thrilled her. Pip smiled as it sank in that she didn't have to be so afraid with this man. That he wanted her for her and would never do anything she didn't like.

And that made all the difference.

Pip leaned forward and pressed her lips against his.

Matt didn't rush her, didn't push for more than she was ready to give. He just held her, touched her, let her touch him, until he was missing his shirt and her blouse was undone and for the first time in her life Pip was making out with a man she wanted.

It was Matt who finally called a halt, when they heard the sound of a big engine outside.

Pip kissed him one more time and righted her blouse, just in time to be greeted by her eldest sister.

Despite Jay Gunderson, it had been one of the best nights she'd experienced in a very long time.

43

Pɪᴘ ᴅɪᴅɴ'ᴛ ɢᴇᴛ ᴛᴏ ꜱᴇᴇ Mᴀᴛᴛ ꜰᴏʀ ᴛᴡᴏ ᴅᴀʏꜱ. Mostly because the entire county was practically in riots after a virus struck half the cattle in the county. It was curable, but it meant every vet and tech—Matt and his people, plus those from the surrounding three counties—were run ragged.

He'd made a point of calling her before she'd gone to bed both nights. Just to talk. Pip had never had a guy do that, and it had felt weird at first. But only at first; within two minutes, she was just fine. Perci had ragged at her for two days, just teasing her in general.

But today when she'd come out of the barn

from feeding Wind Lover, he had been there. Waiting.

There was a tall handsome man waiting on her porch, a bouquet of zinnias clutched tightly in his hand. It wasn't a store-bought bouquet, of that she had no doubt. In fact, it looked like he may have helped himself to some of the zinnias Phoebe had planted along the walk before she moved out.

He only had half a dozen or so, but if her sister ever found out that he had been the one...well, Matt would be in serious trouble. "Those are Phoebe's flowers, Matt. She's not going to be happy with you."

"Then she'll have to be unhappy with her goats. I found a couple of them loose when I came up. These were the only flowers that survived. And I figured rather than let them go to waste, or become a snack later, I'll give them to the most beautiful girl in the world. So...here you go."

She knew he was full of it, but Pip's cheeks still turned red. She held out a hand and took the flowers gently. No man had ever given her flowers, even those rescued from goats before. She'd treasure the gnawed-on flowers for the rest of her life. "Why are you here today, doctor?"

"To see what you are doing this evening."

"Well, Phoebe and Joel are coming over to get the boys. I've got them packing a bag each right now. Parker and Patton, especially, are missing Phoebe. I think they said something about watching kids' movies over at your house tonight. Those yellow Twinkie-looking characters, I think."

"I'm not asking about the boys. I want to know what *you* have planned for after they leave."

"I don't know. I am probably going to do some laundry, do some weeding in the garden. Phoebe used to take care of it, but she hasn't had much time for it lately."

"How about if I help you with the weeding quickly, and then you allow me to take you into Masterson and buy you dinner? Rumor has it they're hanging up a sheet next to the community center and going to show one of that moron Bowles's latest films; since he's a local celebrity now and everything. They like him and are cele-brating he's chosen Masterson. Pitiful."

"You want me to go with you." He wanted her specifically to go on a date with him. It wasn't a family thing. It wasn't her getting a ride. It wasn't anything other than a man asking a woman on a date. And there wasn't a moment's hesitation or a moment of fear.

She wanted to be with Matt.

And that's all it was.

She trusted the man in front of her enough to finally not be afraid.

Pip almost forgot how to breathe as the enormity of that sank in.

44

Pip had a great time. And she had to admit the movie was one she greatly enjoyed. Rowland Bowles was an exceptionally talented director; everyone knew that. She could see why the town of Masterson had greeted him with open arms.

That didn't mean she wanted to be in his movie. The mere thought of it was enough to break her out in hives. Public speaking of any kind was just too much for her. It had been enough for her when people stopped her and Matt and asked which twin she was.

How was she supposed to make Rowland Bowles understand that? He'd shown up twice since the dance. And she was certain she saw him across the crowd at the diner, eyeing her. Eyeing her and Matt with a strange sort of intent.

Matt led her to the back booth and took the seat across from her. "You have an admirer. Bowles is having a hard time keeping his eyes off of you."

"He's relentless about that movie. He's shown up twice since the dance. This last time he offered me a lot of money to do it. I just can't."

"Don't let him force you into doing anything. He gets too pushy, send him to me. I'll fill him in on the way of things around here."

"I can handle him, Matt. But the offer is appreciated. I don't know why he wants me instead of Perci, anyway. She could do what he wanted. Easily. But he insists it's not her that he wants, that it's me; but that doesn't make any sense to me. It's not like we're not identical or anything, after all. He likes the way I look. Well, Perci looks just the same."

"When a man stares at you long enough, baby, he sees the differences. Your sister is a remarkably beautiful woman, yes. And, yes, you are identical. But there's something about you that sets you apart. It's that something that Bowles wants. Hell, it's that something that's kept me from ever confusing the two of you. Nate, too. I don't think he's ever mistaken the two of you, either. You are you, not Perci; just like Perci's Perci and not you. I see that. Nate sees that. I think Bowles is probably wiser than he appears. He sees it, too. We both saw you the night of Phoebe and Joel's wedding. The way you flew across the field. Breathtaking. A man knows what he wants when he sees it, sees her."

"What do you want from me, Matt? Because you changed after Phoebe and Joel's wedding, too. Didn't you? I mean, the dance, then tonight. The way you look at me."

Matt leaned forward, and then he took her hands in his. "Baby, there's something you need to understand. I have always looked at you the way I'm looking at you right now. From the moment I bought those horses and you and Perci rode in on Wind Dancer and Air Dancer, I have looked at you and no other. Pulling you out of the river that day just cemented what I already knew with one look. It's you I'm looking at, Philippa Tyler, and no one else. What you want to do about it, is up to you, but it's not going to change how I feel."

45

Jay sat in his booth at the diner and boiled with rage. She was with him again.

That Masterson bastard. Why was she with him? Didn't she see that Masterson was just another prick who would use her for sex and then drop her when he was finished? Masterson was a few years older than Jay, and like all his brothers, he'd had a steady stream of women in his life. And he'd not been serious about any of them. What would make him be so serious about Pip?

Masterson was using her. It was clear to him. Why wasn't it clear to her?

Jay wanted to rush over to that table she shared with that bastard and yank her away. Protect her. Let her know that she didn't need a man like Masterson.

That she had *him*.

Instead he forced himself to calmly walk out of the diner, as if he hadn't seen them, and head out to the old truck his father had kept for him while he'd been in jail.

Instead of heading home, though, he headed to her place. Just to see what she loved, to smell her.

To plan.

46

Matt took her back to his place with him. Pip knew she'd surprised her sisters when she'd arrived, but she didn't care. Phoebe looked at her with a question in her blue eyes, but Pip just shook her head. Pan made a snarky comment about something being in the Masterson water.

Pip said nothing in response. She wasn't the least bit embarrassed to be with the man next to her.

She never would be.

Instead she helped herself to some leftover popcorn and gummy worms—Parker's favorite treat—and settled at the dining room table in Matt's house.

All four brothers lived there, but it was just a temporary arrangement. Matt and Levi both had other properties they were refurbishing nearby. This was the family homestead, even though their mother didn't live there with them any longer.

This was where Matt grew up. And it was where Phoebe's children would grow up.

It was a beautiful place. She could see what about it had attracted Rowland Bowles.

The boys were all asleep, and she didn't even try to move them. There was no point in it.

Instead, she let Matt drive her home. Perci had worked a half shift and was waiting for her. When she kissed Matt good night on the front porch, she knew something had changed between them once again.

And it was a change she would never regret.

PAN SHOWED UP AN HOUR AFTER PIP HAD finally taken a break the next day. She needed to drive into town and stop by Matt's office to pick up an antibiotic for Air Dancer.

Matt had taken a look at the horse that morning when she'd asked, stopping by on his way into town. He'd said it was because he wanted to check on Wind Lover, but she knew the truth.

His kisses hadn't lied.

It was just a matter of time before they took the next step.

Pip was ready.

She'd had a long discussion with Perci about that very eventuality the night before. Her sister had lectured about safe sex and then went into a strange tirade about how that meant the devil was going to be an even greater part of her own life somehow.

Sometimes Perci was weird.

Pip convinced Pan, who was irritated at something Levi had said or done again, to ride into town with her.

She just didn't want to go to town by herself.

They stopped off at the vet clinic and went in. Matt was there, talking with a vet tech and a patient's owner, when she walked in.

He looked up at her and smiled. Pip just stopped walking and smiled back.

"Pitiful. You're as pitiful as Phoebe, Pippy," Pan said.

"Get what we came for, ok?"

Matt finished with his patient and stepped

over to them. He looked at Pan. "Close your eyes, little sister."

Pan obliged. "This is getting ridiculous. Next, it'll be Perci and Nate. I'm putting a hundred pennies on it. Any takers?"

"Hmmm, later," Matt said, right before he swooped down and kissed Pip.

Kissed her for all the world to see. Except her baby sister.

"Sheesh. Come up for air, would ya?"

Pip ignored her sister. Pip just kissed him back.

47

JAY HAD FOLLOWED HER AND THAT BLONDER sister of hers into town, making sure to keep distance between her truck and his. It had just pissed him off when she stopped at that damned vet clinic right away.

She'd driven right to him. Walked right in to him.

Let him kiss her right there in front of the window. Where anyone in the whole damned inbred town could see.

Did she want Masterson to touch her or something? Was she that confused?

Jay found himself driving around the town, just waiting for her. Wondering.

His rage continued to build.

He forced himself to park his truck and go for a walk to fight back some of the anger before he did something stupid. Like shoot out that window and reveal exactly how he felt about the great sonofabitch Matthew Masterson once and for all.

Instead, he found himself walking into a small boutique on Main Street that hadn't been there before he'd been convicted. The woman at the counter was a tall, stacked blonde who smiled at him. "Can I help you?"

Jay didn't recognize her, but she was worth a second look. Not as good as his Pip, but still a good-looking woman. "I'm looking for a gift for my girl."

She smiled. "And what does she like?"

"She loves horses. She has a cream buckskin mare that she really adores."

"I have some horse merchandise in that corner over there. If you need any help, just let me know."

Jay found what he wanted in the bin of stuffed animals and made his purchase.

Before Jay realized what he was doing, he turned his truck back toward Masterson's clinic.

Her orange-and-white truck was still there.

Only that damned Masterson was walking her and her sister over to the diner. He had his arm around Pip, like it belonged there. Like he was shouting to the town that Pip was his.

Instead of Jay's.

Jay turned his truck around and just drove.

Until he ended up right back out at the Tyler ranch.

No one was around, and it was a simple matter of popping a screen off a back window. Within moments, he was inside her house.

He could imagine it smelled like her.

There were four bedrooms on the first floor. and he found hers easily enough. The nurse's room had scrubs in the drawer. Pip's had her jeans and tiny lace and cotton bras. Jay spent a good deal of time with Pip's bras.

As the rest of the afternoon went—and she still didn't return—Jay lost control of the rage consuming him, for the first time since he'd stepped out of prison a free man.

He got back in his truck and pulled out of the Tyler drive, hiding his truck in the grown-over service road where he'd parked it before. He stayed

there until a familiar orange-and-white truck
drove by.

Jay just watched.

48

PAN HAD FINALLY CALMED DOWN OVER WHAT it was that Levi had said to her—Pip hadn't gotten a clear idea what it was, something to do with what a man wanted from a woman or something— and was laughing and teasing Pip about her relationship with Matt.

The only sister who seemed concerned was Perci.

It would always be Perci who worried about her the most.

For some reason, the thought of Perci got stuck in her head. Along with a real feeling of trepidation.

Like something was about to happen.

Pip drove the rest of the way home with one ear tuned to Pan and part of her attention elsewhere. Inward. And outward, in a way few others would understand.

Perci wasn't hurt or anything, Pip would have felt that, but something was *wrong*. Was about to happen.

They pulled into the drive and parked where Pip usually parked. Pan's little two-door was off to one-side where it had always been parked before, and everything looked fine.

Except the front door was standing wide open. Pip was

almost certain she'd closed it. Maybe. She couldn't be certain.

It could have been left ajar and blown open by the wind. It was an extremely windy day. Or Phoebe could have arrived and left it open.

Her oldest sister didn't drive, after all. Phoebe could be inside somewhere and just not have heard them drive up. Phoebe only had sixty percent hearing in one ear, even with her hearing aid. Her oldest sister was completely deaf in the other ear. Sometimes Phoebe just missed things.

Phoebe could even be up with her drove of goats.

So why did Pip feel like that was the wrong answer?

"Pan...something's wrong."

"I know." Her usually bubbly, lively little sister was ghost pale. "What do we do?"

What did they do? What Tylers always did.

They dealt.

But they weren't stupid—they called Libby, the old border collie, from the far barn and kept her with them as they went inside their home. She was older, but fiercely protective. If anyone was in there who didn't belong, Libby would let them know.

Once Pip stepped into the hallway, she knew where the most damage would be. She ordered Pan to stay outside on the porch—not that her sister would listen, but...she had to try.

Pan went straight to the study instead—where their father kept his rifles.

Pan had always been the best shot of the lot of them.

The rest of the house was undisturbed, though someone had taken a cinnamon roll out of the pan. Pan had put them on the counter to cool before she'd left.

None had been missing then.

The toilet seat was up in the downstairs bath-room, the one between her and Perci's rooms. The one she had used right before she and Pan had left.

The seat shouldn't be up.

Pip pulled in a deep breath and opened her bedroom door.

It was as clean as she'd left it.

Except for one thing. A stuffed yellow horse rested on her pillow.

Pan yelled out before Pip could touch it.

Pip forgot about the stuffed horse and ran to-ward her little sister.

What she found had her wanting to lose the lunch that Matt had bought her just two hours earlier.

49

Her shift was only half over, but Perci couldn't shake the feeling that something had happened.

She'd asked Tiff for an extra hour on her lunch break. That would give her time to drive home and check for herself. If her car had just started...but once again, it had given out right when she needed it most.

She had no other option; she knocked on Nate Masterson's office door as hard as she could. It was like nails through her heart to ask that arrogant behemoth for help, but this was for her family. There was nothing she wouldn't do for her family.

He jerked the door open, a clear look of annoyance on his face. Perci didn't give him a chance to say anything. "I need a ride home right now. My car won't start. Hurry!"

He held up a hand and glowered down at her, like always. He would be almost handsome if he didn't glare all the time. But that didn't matter. All that mattered was that he had wheels and could leave whenever he wanted. "Calm down. Tell me what's wrong."

"Pip's in trouble. Right now. I just know it." Perci shoved the panic and fear away as best she could.

"How do you know?"

"I just do. I always know when she's in trouble. I need to get home. Now."

"Let me grab my keys. Call Joel."

"I've already tried. He's out of cell range. Something's *wrong*, Nate, really wrong. Please, hurry."

"I'll get you there. But this better not be some wild-goose chase. And I'm docking your pay until we get back here."

"It isn't a wild-goose chase. It's my sister."

They had just pulled out of the parking lot when his phone rang. He looked at her. Surprise was in his dark green eyes. "It's Pan. Answer it."

Perci did. She listened to her sister's panicked words, fighting off the nausea as her little sister confirmed that something *had* happened. "Nate's driving me home now, Pan. I'll be there as soon as I can. Okay. I understand. Yes, I have money. I'll take care of it. We'll be there as soon as we can. Don't let Pip out of your sight. You have the gun? Good. Don't let her out of your sight. It's her he's after. I just know it. We'll be there when we can. Stay safe and I love you." She disconnected and looked at the man driving her. His expression had darkened at her words. "We need to stop by the general store. I need...I need to buy new underwear."

"Now? What the hell is going on, Perci?"

She shivered—she couldn't stop shivering. Why was this happening again? "Someone broke into our house. He slashed all my underwear into pieces. And he took Pip's. All of hers. Every last pair of her underwear is just gone. I need to buy her new underwear. Before I get home. My sister...we just need new underwear. Can you drive me to the store, please?"

50

PIP WOULD NEVER STOP SHAKING. THE ATTACK had been so damned personal, had hit right in the center of where she felt most vulnerable. Where her twin was most vulnerable, too.

She was glad she wasn't facing this alone. If she had found it all by herself, she didn't know what she would've done. She was grateful Pan was there, but her first instinct had been to call Matt. To have him there next to her, too.

But when she'd dialed his number with Pan's cell phone—Pip didn't carry one of her own—he had been out of range.

Why had someone broken in and taken her underwear?

It didn't make any sense at all. Neither did the destruction to Perci's room. All sorts of thoughts were running through her head. She was just glad Pan was there. They locked the doors and waited. Joel was coming. Joel and some of his people. And Perci—Perci was coming, with Nate.

Phoebe still had the boys over at her house. The boys were safe; it made her sick to even think that this could have happened while her younger brothers were there.

What were they going to do about this? How were they going to find the person responsible? She trusted Joel, of course. She knew he wouldn't stop until he had those answers. Just what had they done this time? They stayed to themselves. Didn't hurt anyone, barely interacted with anyone.

Or maybe that was it; maybe someone didn't like them because they were suddenly a part of the town again? Did they have enemies?

She knew they did.

The Gundersons and the Rutherfords for one thing. Did they have something to do with this? Both Jay Gunderson and John Rutherford were out there. Somewhere. And they hated her family, hated her and Perci, for sure.

Pip barely made it to the back bathroom before she finally lost her lunch.

Pan followed her in there. "I called Phoebe. And Levi. Levi's going to be here in five minutes. He doesn't want us here alone until Joel can get here. Joel's clear across the county. Levi's coming, Pip. We will be okay. I promise we'll find the one who did this. Then we will sic Joel and his brothers on them. How's that sound? They are a pretty scary sight."

Pip washed her face and nodded.

She wanted the answers, wanted the world to be safe again. Was that so much to ask?

51

MATT HAD JUST PULLED IN WHEN LEVI CAME running out of the front door. His brother held a gun in his hands. Not that unusual—rifles were the number one accessory in Masterson County, after all.

Levi didn't stop moving; he ran straight to Matt's truck and hopped in. "What the hell's going on?"

"Get to the Tylers. Now. Some sonofabitch broke in. Pan's over there with Pip now. I don't know what's going on."

Matt didn't question—he just hit the gas.

They were halfway there before he calmed himself down enough to ask what had happened.

"I don't know. Pan called Phoebe. She was afraid, Matt. Someone had broken in and done something to the twins' rooms. I didn't ask for details. I just told her to grab the gun and wait for me there. I told her that I'd be there as soon as I could. Figured you'd feel the same way."

"You're right about that. We sure the guy isn't still there? You call Joel?" Matt refused to let panic take hold. Levi had said she was there with her sister. She was safe.

That something could happen to her and her sister in the meantime hadn't skipped his notice. But he wasn't going to panic.

That ten miles between their place and the Tylers seemed like one hundred. He made it in seven minutes.

Pip and her sister were waiting. Matt jumped from his truck and ran to her. "Pip, baby, come here."

She ran off the porch and threw herself against his chest. Matt closed his arms around her.

He was only barely aware of Levi pulling Pan closer himself.

They just held the sisters for a very long time.

52

PIP KNEW SHE WAS A COWARD. BUT THAT didn't matter in the moment. What mattered was that he was there and she was safe. For one moment she gave in to the fear, the weakness, and just let him hold her. Couldn't she just let him hold her for a little while?

He felt so much stronger than her father. So much stronger than the world. She just wanted him to hold her for a few minutes longer. He seemed to understand that.

He was holding her just as tightly as she was holding him. He didn't pull away until the sheriff's SUV pulled in, lights blazing. Pip's brother-in-law stepped from the cab and rushed across the yard toward them.

"What the hell happened? What's going on? Pip, honey? Pan? Girls, talk to me."

Pip stepped out of Matt's arms and looked at her brother-in-law. "When we got home, Pan and I noticed that the door was wide open. We called the dog then came inside and checked the house."

"That ever happens again you are to get back in your car and drive straight to our place, no hesitation," Joel ordered. "Anytime something happens, you understand?"

Pip nodded. But this was their house. Not the Mastersons. It was her home, hers and her father's and Perci's and the boys; their home had been violated. They had every right to go inside.

But they would discuss that later. Joel needed to know what they'd find inside. "We went inside and checked the house. Someone had been in there. He left the toilet seat up and ate one of our cinnamon rolls. Perci's room took the most damage. Someone dumped her dresser on the floor. He cut her bras and panties into pieces. They're all ruined. My room..."

"What did they do in yours?" Matt asked. He was still next to her, his hand on her shoulder. He pulled her back so that she could rest against his chest while she faced his brother.

"My top drawer was open. My underwear is gone; it's nowhere in the house. My entire top drawer was empty. We did laundry yesterday; everything but what I'm wearing now was in that drawer. And now it's gone. Perci's is destroyed. Why would he do that? Why did he do that?"

Joel stepped closer and put his hands on her cheeks. Her sister's husband kissed her lightly on the forehead. "I don't know, baby, but I'm going to find out. I can promise you that."

"Tell them about the rest of it, Pip," Pan said from next to Levi.

"What else?" Matt asked from behind her.

"There was a stuffed horse on my pillow. Yellow, with black points and a pink hair bow. We didn't touch it. But I know it's not mine. We've never seen it before. And in the middle of Perci's bed was one of our kitchen knives. Jammed right into the center of where my sister sleeps."

53

MATT LOOKED AT HIS OLDER BROTHER, SEEING the same fury he felt in Joel's eyes. It was a clear threat against the twins. They were the only sisters living here now. But what did it mean?

Matt didn't have a clue; he was a vet, not a cop.

"Joel, any ideas what this means?"

"It damn well means she's not staying here tonight alone," Joel said.

"Perci's on her way home. Nate's bringing her," Pan said. "I'm not sure why he's bringing her, but he is. She's not alone. They should be here any minute."

"That doesn't matter. The twins are not

staying here tonight."

"I can't leave Wind Lover," Pip said. "Or the rest of the horses. It's me and Perci here right now until Dad gets back. Someone has to stay with our livestock."

She looked up at him like he would have all the answers. But Matt didn't. All he had was the anger. And the fear. "Don't worry, baby. I'm staying, too. I'm not leaving you and your sister here alone."

Matt put his arm around her from behind, resting his hand over her stomach. He pulled her closer. Just breathed her in. Reassured himself that she was safe and right there in front of him. What if she and Pan had arrived while the sonofabitch was there? What would they have done then?

They had the rifle, but he knew the truth.

They were practically defenseless against a man his size. Against a man of any size. They'd fight—he had no doubt that the Tylers would fight —but they would lose. They were just too damned small to defend themselves all that well.

Pip shocked the hell out of him when she leaned back against him. Let him hold her. When her hand wrapped around his arm.

She just stayed there while they watched Nate's truck pull up the drive.

Pip's twin hopped out of the passenger seat and ran up the steps. Matt felt Pip start to shake in his grasp. He let her go. She threw herself at her identical sister, and the two of them clung together. Probably much the same way they'd been doing since birth.

Matt looked at Nate as his brother followed behind Perci. The fury was hard to miss on Nate's face, as well.

It was obvious that Perci was just as frightened as the other two sisters. And why wouldn't she be? She had been just as violated as Pip. Why had someone done this to these women? That's what Joel was going to have to find out. Matt was going to ride his brother's ass until he did.

"I need to see, girls," Joel said. "But I don't want you touch anything."

"There's not much to see in Pip's room," Pan said. "It's as neat in there as always. Except her top drawer is open. And the stuffed horse. Watching everything. Perci's room is where the real mess is."

"I need to see for myself," Perci said. There was determination in her face. And fear. It hurt

Matt to look at her, seeing how much she resembled Pip. It was like seeing Pip's fear doubled.

Nate practically hovered over Perci as they all walked down the narrow hall that led to the bedrooms.

The Tyler house wasn't overly large, and it was crowded. Levi and Pan had stayed outside.

Matt was there when Nate and Perci and Joel got the first look at what had been done to Perci's room. Scraps of tattered lace and cotton littered the floor. But it was the big chef's knife jammed through her blankets into the mattress that made the boldest statement.

They crossed the hall; Matt entered Pip's bedroom just after Joel. He'd never been in her space before. It was painted a cool light blue, neat and feminine. And it smelled like her. The top drawer of the old dresser that was in good need of painting stood open. Empty.

It was the only thing out of place in the room.

The eighteen-inch stuffed horse, soft yellow with a black mane, almost looked as if it belonged on Pip's pillow.

If they had not mentioned the stuffed animal, he never would've known that it wasn't hers.

To Matt, that horse was more of a threat than anything else had been.

Why would someone go to all of the trouble of vandalizing one twin's room and leaving a cute gift in the other's?

Levi took Pan back to their place. She hadn't wanted to go, but Levi had pulled the dirty card. Reminded her that she had work to do. Told her he was her boss, after all.

It was not exactly how Matt would've done it, but it was effective. It got the youngest Tyler sister back to where she was safe, at least. Which had been Levi's objective in the first place. They all knew that—except possibly Pip and her sisters. He wished Pip would go back with his brother, too. Let Matt stay with the livestock. Pip would be safe that way.

He knew better than to even suggest it.

There was no way in hell he was leaving her there without him. Perci actually thanked Nate for the ride home, standing close to Nate.

That told Matt exactly how frightened Perci was. And why wouldn't she be?

Someone had driven a twelve-inch knife through her bed. The place where a woman was the most vulnerable. The bastard had violated it on purpose. It made him wonder if the threat was actually against Perci? Anyone who knew anything about her would know that threatening one of her sisters would terrify Perci.

Had Pip just been collateral? Had someone been trying to get even with Perci for some perceived slight? It was possible; but it didn't sound likely to him.

It was the stuffed animal that worried him the most. The horse looked too much like Wind Lover, right down to the sweet face.

What did that tell them? That someone had been close enough to Pip to see that horse, to go to a store somewhere and buy the stuffed version. Or order it off the internet and wait for it to be shipped—how long had that person been watching her?

Maybe it was Pip, and Perci was the collateral?

To get that particular horse, someone had to have been close enough to Pip to know she was the one connected to the real horse and not Perci. To know that Perci's room was the pink one and Pip's the blue.

No, Matt knew it in his gut.

It was Pip that the sonofabitch wanted.

54

Matt walked out with Joel hours later. Joel had called in a crime-scene tech from eighty miles away, and the young guy had dusted for prints and DNA on the knife and on the toilet. On Pip and Perci's dressers. It would take a while, but they might get an answer that way.

Matt discussed his theories and concerns with his brother, as Joel grabbed a duffel bag with extra clothes out of the back of his SUV and tossed it at him.

"The horse says someone has been close to her." Joel's concern was in the green eyes he'd inherited from their father like all of Matt's brothers. "But the rage was definitely directed at Perci."

"Find him, Joel. Before I do. Hell, before Nate does." His slightly younger brother had made how he felt about the person responsible very clear.

"I suggest we let Nate find him. Little brother is pissed. And I understand it." Joel looked back up at the house, now alight with warmth. Matt knew what his brother saw. It had been painted, but it was still an older house. The people inside didn't deserve this terror.

"You think it's John Rutherford?"

"It makes the most sense. Either him or that idiot Jay Gunderson. Though rumor has it Gunderson's just spending his time out on his ranch fixing it up. Seems determined. And they let him out on good behavior, Matt. It's most likely Rutherford. He's been seen in the area."

"Find him, damn it."

"I'm doing the best I damned well can. You just watch your back. And hers."

"Better believe I will. If I have my way, she'll be moving with me to the Hodsen homestead as soon as the floors are replaced." He hadn't put his wishes into place in his head until that moment, but it was what he wanted.

Pip. In his future, indefinitely. Forever.

"Knew the wind blew that way."

"What can I say? I've practically loved her since the moment I fished her out of a river in time to save your sorry ass."

"Yeah. Tyler women are like that. All it takes is one look for them to crawl under your skin and stick forever. Levi and Nate don't have a chance. It's just a crapshoot about who will fall first."

55

JAY HAD FOUND HIMSELF A GOOD PLACE TO hide, and he cursed himself for being stupid. He'd come back.

He'd regretted what he'd done less than an hour after he'd done it. He'd decided to go see for himself that she was all right.

He'd known that was stupid. He'd seen her come home.

He had stuck around and watched as she and her sister had come outside, rifles in hand.

They'd been so scared because of what he had done. He shouldn't have scared them like that—he remembered what it was like to be that frightened of things.

Jay had hidden and watched as those damned Mastersons had shown up.

As they'd held her and her sisters. As those Mastersons had held their girls, as those Mastersons had had women who mattered to them. Who they mattered to.

Rage and envy had boiled in him until he'd totally lost control of himself.

He'd retreated to the second barn and planned. Planned exactly what he was going to do. He was going to have to get a distraction going, and then he was going to get his girl. Once and for all.

After that he was going to take her to his hunting cabin for a while. It was where he was staying until he could get his ranch remodeled. The floor needed to be completely replaced—it wasn't safe for his girl just yet. He could have stayed with his daddy, but things had changed when Jay had asked his daddy what he'd said to Pip that night. When Clint had told Jay quietly what rumors were going around, about how Pip's Mama had died.

Poor girl; his daddy had had no business doing that to her. To *her*. Jay's *girl*.

His father also hadn't liked Jay questioning him. That had been obvious.

He hadn't realized his daddy had a beef with Phil Tyler, either. But the older man did.

Jay didn't have time to wonder, though. He had another five gallons of gasoline to deal with.

56

MATT WALKED BACK TO THE FRONT DOOR OF the Tyler ranch with determination, Joel's words fresh in his mind.

If he wanted that woman safe, keep her that way. He'd heard the frustration at the lack of answers in Joel's words. And he'd understood. His brother wanted Pip safe. Period.

But there were rules that Joel had to follow.

Rules Matt didn't.

Matt walked into the house and kept walking until he found Perci and Nate in the kitchen. Perci looked so pale, so frightened.

Matt knelt down in front of this woman with Pip's face.

"I'm here to stay. I'm staying until Joel catches the guy. I'm not leaving Pip—or you—until we have him."

"And what does my sister think of this?" Perci looked at him, questions in those eyes of hers. It was like looking at Pip, but it wasn't. A rush of emotion for this sister of the woman he loved shot right through him.

"I haven't told her yet. I'm just here. And I'm staying here until I'm sure the two of you are safe."

He might have been mistaken, but he was certain he saw the relief in her eyes. But Perci would never admit to being afraid, would she? "I see."

"Where is Pip?" She should have been right there. But wasn't.

"Barn, where else? She took her rifle, though." Nate said, pointing out the window. "She's more stubborn than the rest of them, your girl. I argued for five minutes, and she never budged, just insisted with the deputy out there she was fine—and I should stay with her sister."

"It isn't enough. You should have called me back in." He'd called after speaking with Joel and arranged things with his head vet tech. Derrick would handle any appointments or calls that he could and direct the rest to Matt out at the Tyler ranch. If he had to go to town on a call, he'd be bringing Pip into town with him. It wouldn't be ideal for her, but it was a solution he was more comfortable with.

"Didn't think it was; it's why I'm still here, watching. I need to head back into town. I left the hospital in a real lurch. I need to get back. Deputy just went behind the far barn."

"Go. I have things covered. And thanks, Nate." He was keeping her safe. Period.

57

Jay heard the barn door open, and he jerked behind the corner of the nearby shed just as the buckskin mare and her foal were released into the paddock. He got a glimpse of the woman he was after before she was cut off from his view by that damned vet Masterson.

Jay pushed back the immediate rage. Matt Masterson's time was coming. Jay had promised himself that.

No man would touch his Pip and live.

He waited to give them time to get out of the barn. He hadn't planned on Masterson being there. It would take him a while to figure out how to deal with the guy.

Masterson wasn't a punk kid like Phoenix Tyler. Masterson was actually a lot bigger.

That hadn't kept Jay from fighting before. He'd taken care of the deputy wandering the place with a simple knock to the head with a damned rock he'd found. Guy had gone down without a sound—or a fight. Pitiful.

Jay moved faster.

He dumped the rest of the gas around the bottom back of the barn. He hadn't dumped any inside yet.

He was hoping the breeze would take the smell downwind, until he got things into place like he wanted.

It wasn't the biggest barn on the Tyler ranch, but it would be one hell of a distraction.

Masterson would probably rush right out there to fight the fire. Anyone else would, too.

Masterson would make sure Pip stayed back. Safe from the flames.

Jay had waited long enough—he slipped in the back door of the barn.

He had his cigarettes and lighter in his pocket. As soon as he found the right moment, the barn was as good as gone.

And Pip was going to be his.

58

MATT FOUND HER IN THE BARN, SECONDS after she sent Wind Lover and the foal into the pasture. She had the rifle leaning against the stall.

When Matt walked in, Pip paused and looked over at him. "Matt, I needed to see to the horses."

"You should have waited for me. Joel and I discussed it, and I need to stay here until we find out who's responsible. He's putting a deputy in a car outside your house for tonight once he gets here, but I need to stay here with you. I can't not be here."

He knew better than to force her to do anything. And he would never do that to her. Never take her choices away from her. He understood that that was an important component of who she was. Of who they were going to be together. He hadn't explained himself very well, had he?

"I can't not be here, baby, any more than Joel could ever leave Phoebe."

"Why?" Her lips trembled as she spoke. He followed her out of the stall. Forcing himself not to just reach out and touch her. Once they were clear of the stall, she turned to him. He watched her swallow. Watched her wrap her arms over her stomach and looked at him directly. Tension twisted his gut.

Now wasn't exactly how he wanted to have this conversation with her, was it? No, Matt had half thought it would be with them cuddled together after loving each other.

"Why do you think?" It was confrontation time, wasn't it? It was time he laid himself bare, put it all out there, for her to understand.

"I don't know. I don't understand you. I think I'm starting to, but I can't be for certain. How do you feel about me, Matt? I need to know the truth right now. There has to be honesty. What do you want from me? Are you just here because of what happened to my underwear? Or do you feel what I am starting to?"

Matt said to hell with it, and he wrapped his hands around her waist. His trembling hands. When had that happened? When had this woman gotten so deeply under his skin that this very moment would matter so much? He didn't know the exact moment; he just knew that it had.

"I want everything from you, Philippa Marie Tyler. Everything you are willing to give. But I am an impatient man, and I'm struggling with it. I know you need soft and quiet and gentle and easy...and slow, but I'm not sure I can do that. You burn me, and it takes everything I've got to hold back the flames. Do you understand what I'm saying?"

She was silent for the longest moment, and Matt knew he'd blown it. He'd scared her away completely. She was going to tell him he was crazy and to stay far away from her. That was going to be the end of it for both of them.

And then she shocked the hell out of him when she reached out. One small hand slid up his chest and rested on the back of his neck.

And then Pip leaned closer.

59

IT HAD BEEN THE NERVES, THE VULNERABILITY on his face and in his words that had made up her mind for her.

No more being a coward. Pip was done being afraid of everything. Being afraid of him. Matt would never hurt her.

For the first time, she realized that she could be the one hurting him. And that was the last thing she ever would've wanted. "Kiss me again, Matt. Just kiss me again, right here."

He did. Exactly as she wanted. His hands tightened around her waist, and he lifted her off her feet. Pip knew exactly what he wanted her to do. And she did it. She wrapped her legs around his waist until she could feel him pressed up against her. Until he was holding her pressed up against him.

One of his hands slipped up and knocked the hat off her head. It fell to the barn floor practically unnoticed. And then his hand was tangled in her hair, and he was holding her still, as his mouth fused to hers. And as she kissed him back just as hungrily.

It was her that slipped open that first button. Her that slipped his shirt off his broad shoulders. He didn't wear anything underneath it. No undershirt for him. It was just too damned hot outside for that. She spread her fingers wide over the most perfect male chest she had ever seen.

His heart pounded beneath her hand. Telling her exactly how much the man wanted her.

Her, Philippa Tyler. No one else. She was not second best for him. He hadn't seen Perci first and decided to settle on second best.

He'd seen her, and he'd wanted her.

But it was more than that. It was in his kindness, his loyalty, his bravery, his gentleness, the love he had for his family; it was in the way she trusted him. And it was in the way he looked at her. "Pip? How far are you wanting us to go? Because, baby, I'm a man holding the woman I want. You have to know that there is nothing I wouldn't give to just lay you down there on that hay where we've slept together before. Show you exactly how much I do want you. But it's got to be your choice, Pip. Yours. So if you want me to stop, now's the time to say it. You just tell me what you want, baby."

Pip pulled in a deep breath and stared at him. He let go of her hip, and she slid her legs back to the ground. She stepped away from him, but not too far.

His breath caught.

She knew what he was thinking in that very moment. Pip swallowed and looked at him. Knew that what she was about to do was going to change everything between them. Forever.

Her hands went to the bottom of her shirt, and she lifted, pulling it over her head. And tossing it to the hay next to them. "I don't want you to stop, Matt. I don't want you to ever stop looking at me or touching me the way you do."

He reached for her and scooped her into his arms. Pip caught her breath as a soft laugh slipped out. It was easy to forget what had happened inside when she was with him. Matt made her forget the fear. And she suspected he always would.

"That saddle blanket still around here?"

"Right where you left it the last time you were here. It's just been waiting." Just like she had been, and that was more than clear to her now. Pip leaned forward and pressed her lips to his.

60

JAY STOOD IN THE STALL AND LISTENED TO THE sounds of that bastard Matt Masterson holding and cuddling Pip. It was obvious what they'd just finished doing—in the damned barn, of all places. With a deputy walking around and her sister inside the house.

Had she no shame?

His Pip had given herself to that Masterson without hesitation. Because she wanted him. She was no better than those sisters of hers, was she? That little slut had wanted a Masterson. Instead of him.

All these years he had waited for her, had

been confident in the fact that she was waiting for him.

But she hadn't been.

She'd been screwing around with the first sonofabitch that had looked at her. How long had she been with Masterson? How long had she been whoring herself for him? Was she only after what Masterson could give her?

This place, this damned Tyler ranch, was obviously a shit hole. Not fit for rats to live in, let alone humans. But here she was. Her and that twin of hers and those younger brothers. It was filthy, run-down, poor, and disgusting. Was that what this was about?

Was she, like her oldest sister, whoring herself to a Masterson to pay her way through life? Was she that desperate?

What was it Masterson could give her that Jay couldn't?

Jay fought the rage that continued to build and build. Until he had completely lost the battle.

He grabbed the shovel by the handle and waited. Waited until the damned sonofabitch had pulled his jeans back up, waited until Pip had redressed herself. Waited until they were cuddled there on the hay, Masterson whispering soothing words as he stroked her side. As they spoke quietly.

As Pip thanked Masterson. *Thanked him* for screwing her. Was she that hard up?

And then he heard his own name. Heard her talking about how he had terrified her for so long. How she was afraid she would never heal after what that monster had done to her.

What had he done to her?

Except get a little too carried away? But surely she understood that he was angry that day, that he was drunk, and young, and immature? That it wouldn't be like that between them now.

Jay dropped his lit cigarette to the hay. Then the rest of the damned pack right on top of it. He waited, just long enough for the flames to grow a bit.

He had to make her see. Make her see that he was the better man than that damned vet. He had to make her see. He pushed open the stall door and stepped up behind where that damned Masterson knelt over her.

Pip saw him, and her hands tightened on Masterson's chest. She screamed.

Jay acted. He brought the shovel down on

Masterson's head quickly, but the sonofabitch turned at the last second.

Masterson went down, out cold on the blanket they'd just screwed on. Jay tossed the shovel aside, though he wanted to pick it up and just pound the shit out of Masterson. Crack his head open. But he didn't have time for that.

He reached down and grabbed Pip. She fought and fought.

Jay had no choice. He pulled back his fist and struck her. Dazing her. She fell to the ground.

He made himself a vow: that was the last time he would ever strike her. Ever. But it was necessary. He had to do what he had just done. He slung her over his shoulder; she was so small it was easy to do. Jay ran out the back of the barn.

And straight into that damned director, Rowland Bowles.

61

ROWLAND HAD HAD A BIT TOO MUCH WINE the night before, once the rest of his production crew had arrived. It was the hangover that had made Rowland sluggish that afternoon when they'd driven out to the Tyler ranch.

Jenny hadn't had too much, though—apparently his newest assistant was a little teetotaling Puritan. One who had assigned herself the Herculean task of keeping Rowland under control. Rowland wanted to act out, just to give sweet little Jenny something to do with her time. She was so fun in her serious nerdy way. Rowland looked over at her, admiring the way the jeans she wore fit her tiny apple-shaped bottom.

She was so small and curvy and so damned innocent; he'd dreamed of her all night long. Of making her less than innocent.

She had no business in his dreams at night.

Jenny screamed. The sound went straight through Rowland's head.

Someone else yelled, and he turned quickly to see what it was that had terrified Jenny.

A madman was coming right toward them—carrying a screaming Tyler twin over his shoulder.

"Bowles! Matt's in the barn! Fire! Help!"

The terror broke through his hangover quickly. Rowland glanced toward the barn—flames were rapidly devouring it. And Masterson was in there?

Jenny figured it out far faster than Rowland, to his shame.

His scrappy little assistant yelled and jumped at the man holding the twin, trying to free the Tyler sister.

It didn't happen.

Rowland watched in horror as the sonofabitch swung out—sending Rowland's sweet little Jenny tumbling to the ground.

Rowland growled and lunged at the smaller

man, fury unlike any he'd ever felt before filling
him.

62

PIP HAD NEVER BEEN SO HAPPY TO SEE someone like Rowland Bowles before in her life. Terror filled her when the director dove at Jay, when Jay's hand loosened around her arm.

Matt.

All she could think about was Matt.

Pip ran for the small barn, hoping, praying she could get to him. Hoping she wasn't already too late.

Someone screamed her name from the porch. She knew who it was. She'd always know when it was Perci. Always.

Pip didn't stop. The door was wide open, and flames were shooting out toward the hayloft above.

Matt—Matt had fallen near the back, near Wind Lover's stall. As she rushed into the barn, that was where she headed.

To Matt.

Pip couldn't see anything; smoke rolled around them. But she knew this barn. She'd been in it every single day of her life. She used instinct and memory to guide her to where she'd last seen the man that she loved.

For Pip trust had had to come first. And it had. There was no man in the world she trusted as much as she had Matt Masterson; and she knew it. Matt had somehow quietly become her world in a way she didn't fully understand yet.

She wanted to. She wanted to have the opportunity to know.

"Matt! Matt! Where are you?"

63

Matt smelled the smoke the moment he regained control of his senses. It took him a moment to remember what had happened—and he still wasn't certain of what it had been.

He'd been with Pip.

Pip.

Who was yelling his name. Matt forced his eyes open. Fire and smoke was everywhere. The hay beneath him was engulfed—only a foot of unburned hay remained around his head and arms, his body.

Matt jumped to his feet, clutching his head and trying to ignore the pain in his left arm and shoulder.

It was broken.

He had no doubt about that. But he would deal with that later. He had to find her, had to get out of there.

"Pip! Where are you?"

"Here!" Small hands wrapped around his left and he bit back a curse at the rush of pain. "We have to get outside!"

"Hang on." He wrapped his good arm around her and started toward where he thought the door was. "Let's get out of here together!"

"This way! The back door is closer!"

Matt couldn't orient himself—not with the pain in his shoulder and head and the darkness of the smoke. "You'll have to lead the way, baby. I can't see, and I don't know the way!"

64

PERCI HEARD THE SCREAMING ONLY SECONDS after she got that feeling—the one that told her Pip was in trouble. That voice that told her Pip needed her. She turned off the shower and grabbed her pajamas—she'd needed a shower and a good cry—and threw them on.

Pip needed her.

And Perci could already smell the smoke.

She ran out the back door, knowing her sister and Matt would be near the horses and Phoebe's goats if there was something wrong.

Perci ran around the corner of the larger barn toward the small one at the back where the smoke billowed.

Wind Lover was screaming, the fire terrifying the little buckskin and her foal.

But it was the sight of her sister running toward the open barn door and practically diving into the flames that had the same terror freezing Perci to her soul.

"Pip!"

Perci kept running, past the men fighting in her side yard. She recognized them both, but she didn't stop.

Perci headed toward the small barn right after her sister.

65

For the first time in a long while, Rowland didn't know what to do. He lay stunned on the sparse grass for a moment then rolled to his side. He had to do something.

Jenny pulled herself to her feet and looked around wildly. Her hands were on her head, and Rowland saw blood. He lurched to his feet and went to her. "Let me see, Jenny. Just let me see."

"What happened?"

What had happened? She'd jumped a man more than a foot taller than she was to protect a virtual stranger. Brave girl. But maybe not so bright. "Some guy hit you then jumped me."

"He had one of those girls with him. He was going to hurt her, wasn't he? Where is she?"

Pip. The man, Gunderson, had had her, hadn't he?

Maybe. It could have been Perci. Rowland wasn't so sure.

Rowland looked up just as two small women ran toward the burning barn.

"Go!" Jenny pulled at his arm. "Go! You have to help them!"

Rowland looked at her. "I can't leave you."

"Please, I've been taking care of myself for twenty-five years. I don't need someone like you. But they just might. Go!"

Rowland went.

66

THEY COULD SEE DAYLIGHT. MATT PUSHED her ahead of him. "Go!" He coughed, knowing they only had a few more moments before one or the other of them was overcome by smoke. "Get out, Pip! Go!"

Something slammed into him, knocking him to the ground. Matt jerked when his left arm landed in burning straw. He yelled out.

"You can't have her!" the man yelled. Matt knew who it was, though it was hard to see anything in the rolling smoke.

He didn't waste time talking; Matt drove his good arm into the man's face. Gunderson went down with a scream.

Matt was at a disadvantage—his shoulder was broken, he probably had a concussion, and his lungs were damned close to collapsing from everything he'd inhaled.

But Gunderson wasn't going to win.

The man was screaming—screaming for Pip.

The screams of a madman.

Matt grabbed Gunderson's head in his good hand. He shoved the man with everything he had —just as something slammed into Gunderson from the side, sending them both careening.

67

PIP DIDN'T STOP TO THINK. ALL SHE KNEW was that Jay Gunderson was determined to kill Matt. She wasn't about to let that happen. The pitchfork was in her hands before she even realized it. She slammed it against Jay as hard as she could, screaming as she did. She'd thought to grab her father's rifle, but it was surrounded by flames now.

Useless.

The deputy wasn't going to be any help—she'd jumped over him when she'd gotten closer to the barn. She didn't know if Jay had killed him or not.

The fire...the back of the barn was completely

engulfed. They weren't going to be able to make it out the rear of the building, no matter what.

Matt stumbled to the side, almost going down to the dirt floor. He was hurt; she just knew that. The same way she would know if Perci was hurt.

Because she loved him.

Loved him so much.

"Matt! Come on!" She reached for him—just as someone grabbed her and yanked her off her feet.

Someone strong and male and screaming her name.

Screaming his rage.

Jay.

Choking her. Screaming that she was a lying whore. A slut. His.

Pip reached up and clawed where she thought the man's eyes were.

She got lucky. He screamed and knocked her to the ground.

Matt lunged over her, taking Jay to the floor. They grappled, rolling far too close to the growing flames.

They had to get out of there, fast.

Someone else was there, grabbing for her. Pulling her to her feet.

"Pip, come on. We need to get out of here!"

Perci; of course, it would be Perci.

"Get out, Perci! Get help! Go!" She wanted to grab her twin, pull her sister to safety. Push her out the door to Rowland Bowles or the second deputy who was supposed to be on his way.

But she couldn't leave Matt. She wouldn't.

Pip dove at the two men, wrapping her arm around Jay's neck and tightening. She yanked at his hair. "Let him go!"

She wasn't leaving this barn without the man she loved.

68

PERCI DOVE FOR JAY'S LEGS AS HER SISTER dove for his head.

Pip went wild, yanking on Jay's hair and ears, clawing at his eyes and mouth, biting like a feral cat. Anything she could to get him off Matt.

Matt pulled himself to his feet.

Perci could barely see him, but he was bloodied and covered in soot. And reaching for her sister.

Jay kicked out, catching Perci in the chin. She saw stars for a moment.

It was enough for him to throw Pip off. She landed in a pile of hay—hay that was igniting. Pip screamed and threw the hay off her arms.

Something crackled overhead, loud and terrifying.

Perci looked up in time to see one of the support beams burning in two. Any moment it was going to fall.

On her sister below.

Perci yelled and dove for her twin.

69

MATT WATCHED IT HAPPEN; HIS SCREAM blended in with the twins'.

He grabbed Gunderson by one arm and shoved the man as hard as he could to the ground. Gunderson's head bounced off something hard. The bastard didn't get up again.

Matt turned toward the sounds of Pip screaming for help.

Something knocked into him, and Matt almost went down. This time, though, the man's hands helped him up.

"Masterson! You gotta get out of here, you idiot!"

"Get the twins! Quick! They're hurt!" Matt

didn't stop to question how Rowland Bowles had ended up there; he was just thankful the man had.

He dropped to the dirt floor next to Pip. She was tugging at her sister's arms, trying to pull Perci from beneath a burning beam. Pip wasn't able to get any leverage. Her own legs were pinned beneath her sister. Perci was facedown and not moving. The beam was trapping her beneath it, flames getting closer to the twins by the second.

Matt coughed and grabbed for Perci—she'd have to be moved before he could free Pip. How badly were they hurt?

Bowles wasn't a stupid man—the other guy had started pulling hay from beneath Pip's legs then slid his own arm between Pip's feet.

Matt switched twins; instead of pulling at Perci—who was now crying silently—he wrapped his good hand around Pip's waist from behind and pulled her from beneath her sister.

Just as Bowles yanked Perci free with a Herculean tug that Matt wouldn't have believed if he hadn't seen it himself.

The beam crashed to the dirt floor, sending ash and hay and smoke billowing.

"We need to get out of here!" Bowles yelled.

Gunderson screamed, rage and pain and Pip's name all rolled up into one insane sound.

"I can walk!" Pip yelled. "Just get Perci out!"

"I have her!" Bowles had Perci in his arms. Perci was moving.

"Go!" Matt thought for one split-second of just leaving Gunderson to die. But he couldn't do it. "Get the girls out! We can't leave that bastard to die like this!"

Bowles was already moving, carrying Perci to the barn door fifty feet away.

A small hand wrapped around his. "I'm staying with you!"

Matt wanted to yell at her, tell her to run outside, but they didn't have time to argue. He yanked her closer. "You stay with me!"

"Let's go!"

He stumbled over Gunderson. Literally. Matt caught his balance, barely, with help from Pip. He wrapped his uninjured hand around Gunderson's arm and yanked the man to his feet. "Outside!"

Pip guided him. Matt struggled to drag the fighting man behind him. He was almost ready to say screw it and get Pip out of there instead when Bowles returned.

"Pip! Lead the way!" Matt tried to yell, but the smoke threatened to overtake him.

"Come on, Matt! Come on!"

The three of them pulled Gunderson to the door, and to safety.

"Bowles! Don't let him out of your sight!" Matt turned to Pip, tears streaming out of his eyes.

She reached for him. Just as he reached for her.

He held her until he couldn't fight the darkness any longer.

70

Pip yelled his name when he practically collapsed in her arms. He was covered with soot, and his shirt had charred hole marks all over it. His arm hung awkwardly, and his head was covered with blood.

"Matt!" She tried to get him to open his eyes, but he wouldn't. Pip fought the terror, trying to shove it away.

"Perci! Help him!"

Perci was coughing, sitting forward as Rowland Bowles' assistant tried to wrap her leg in cloth of some sort. Pip looked at her. Some of Perci's hair had been burned off, and she was covered with evidence of the fire, too. Her twin looked almost as bad as Matt. "Is he breathing?"

"Yes."

"Thank God." Perci struggled to pull in air, right before Pip's eyes.

Matt started coughing, and his eyes opened. Pip leaned over him.

His hand reached for her. She held him until help arrived.

When the EMTs on the first chopper ran toward her, that was when Pip moved, letting them help Matt. Pip stood, stepped back. Her knees went out from under her. Pip didn't get up again.

71

Rowland had never experienced anything like what had just happened. He and Jenny were bundled up with the rest of the crowd and transported to the Masterson County hospital moments after the air ambulance had taken off with Masterson and Pip inside.

Perci should have gone with them, but the helicopter hadn't been big enough for three, and she insisted her sister go with Matt.

She'd known the EMTs and flight nurse, and they'd listened when she'd barked out orders at them—around the coughing that had shaken her small body.

Poor kid looked like she'd been through a war. And some of her hair was missing.

He also hadn't missed the bone sticking out of her calf.

Jenny shocked the hell out of him when she took charge of the rest of them. She tied a rope around that bastard Jay Gunderson's hands—then tied him to a fence. When she was finished, she checked on the still unconscious sheriff's deputy and then returned to splinting Perci's broken leg.

The guy just writhed on the grass, screaming for Pip and cursing Matt Masterson's name.

Gunderson hadn't stopped, even when the sheriff and two deputy cars pulled in, sirens blazing, with fire trucks behind them.

When had someone called 911?

Jenny raced to greet them. Of course. There apparently wasn't anything Jenny couldn't handle.

Rowland just stayed where he was, holding little Perci Tyler in his arms as she shook and trembled and coughed. The sheriff ran to her first. "Pip?"

"Perci," Rowland said. And he understood the guy's confusion. The girl's face was covered in black streaks. The same that no doubt covered

Rowland's. "Pip went with the helicopter. She and your brother."

"Joel, we need to get to the hospital. Pip and Matt...they..." Perci stopped talking as more coughing overtook her. "Gunderson tried to kill us all."

Her brother-in-law cursed. He yelled at one of his deputies to get Gunderson to the hospital under guard—without even asking why the man was there in the first place—and then scooped Perci up into his arms. His curses turned the air blue when he saw the damage done to her leg. "What the hell happened?"

"Beam fell on me and Pip," she answered through her tears. "Get me to her, Joel. Just get me there. Please."

"Hold on, baby. I'll get you right there. I promise."

72

PIP FLOATED IN A HAZE OF CONFUSION AS THE EMTs rolled her gurney into the hospital. A tall, massive man stepped close to her. A doctor, and one she recognized. "Honey? Can you hear me? Tell me which twin you are so I know you're in there!"

Matt's brother looked down at her. An immediate feeling of calm took over, brushing aside the panic. Nate would take care of his brother. She lifted one hand to the mask covering her mouth and nose. She pulled it out of her way. "Matt? How's Matt? He was right behind me!"

Nate leaned closer and brushed the hair off her forehead. "That answers that question. He's coming in right behind you, Pip. How badly are you hurt? Can you feel your arms, legs?"

"Yes. Just can't breathe. Ribs. Rafter fell..." Pip remembered it all in that moment. Remembered her sister. "Nate! Perci! *Perci* was with me! The rafter fell on my sister! You have to find Perci! Help her!"

"Shhh. Pip, I'll take care of Perci. I promise."

"Perci and Matt and Jay Gunderson and... please, Nate...please!"

Pip kept pleading and kept calling for Matt and Perci until she was coughing so badly she couldn't speak again.

73

MATT'S EYES OPENED, AND HE LOOKED UP INTO a familiar face. He thought about talking then thought better of it. Only one word escaped around the tube in his damned throat. It was completely garbled, but his younger brother understood.

Nate leaned closer. "Wondered when you were going to rejoin the land of the living."

He tried to say her name again. Nate just sighed and crossed his arms over his chest. "Let me guess. You are going to be just as single-minded as Joel was, aren't you? Pip is doing fine. Minor burns, broken ribs, sprained ankle, smoke inhalation—which was the biggie—and a black eye. Gunderson apparently hit her a time or two. Other than that, she's right there. Sleeping. See?" His brother pointed to the next bed over. "We thought about putting her in with her twin, but Perci said Pip snores, and you get custody of her from now on."

Matt just looked at his brother significantly.

"Perci took a nasty hit across the back from a burning beam, Matt. She's going to have a bit of a scar. She does have six cracked ribs from it. The beam bounced down, we think, and broke her leg. The opposite end caught on part of the back stall that hadn't burned yet, lessening the impact. They got extremely lucky that they were on a pile of hay. It had some give, and at the angle the beam fell, they weren't completely under it. It kept it from landing full on them while burning. Perci will be on crutches for a while—and both are on bronchodilators and a host of other things to repair the smoke damage to their lungs. Same as you. As for you, you took a crack to the head—Pip said a shovel?—a broken clavicle from that shovel, broken ribs, fractured radius in two places, and you and Gunderson beat the hell out of each other. You've had some burns to the throat and mouth. But nothing too serious there. You'll be out of here in a week tops. Just in time for Mother to get back into town and take care of you. She's already called. After what happened to Joel and her being stuck helping out in Mexico with that earthquake...well...she's ready to help her baby boy."

Matt looked at his brother in horror. His mother *hovered* whenever one of her boys was injured. Horribly.

"Yeah, thought that would get your attention." Nate's face darkened. "As for Gunderson, Bowles told us what he saw and what Gunderson did to Bowles's little assistant. Joel also found the remains of a gasoline can inside the barn. Not to mention what the sonofabitch did to the deputy. Guy's going to live, but he got lucky, too. There's a lot of that going around, apparently. Jay Gunderson has been making threats from the moment he was brought in. We have him in a secure room two floors down. Joel and some other officials are waiting on statements from you and the twins. Hell, Matt, I'd only been gone two hours before they were bringing you all in."

Matt wanted the sonofabitch gone. He didn't want Gunderson in the same damned building as Pip. He started to sit up, to look at her for himself. His brother stopped him. "Relax. Joel is working on transferring him to the prison ward eighty miles away. Guy's cuffed to a bed and sedated anyway. He's not getting near her or her sisters again. Levi's sitting in the hallway between your rooms, and Pan's in with Perci."

Matt pulled at the tube in his throat. He wanted it out.

His brother understood. "You turn uncooperative and I'm shoving it right back in."

"Move me closer." Matt's words were harsh and raspy, but Nate understood.

Nate shook his head. "I can't do that. Cords aren't long enough."

"Then get a damned extension cord in here. Get a dozen. Just get my bed right next to hers. I'm going to be the first person she sees when she opens her eyes, Nate. You'd better damned well believe it," he rasped.

"How did I get cursed with the most difficult brothers? Seeing her isn't enough. You have to be practically in the same bed with her? You're as bad as Joel was."

Matt glanced at his brother again, finally taking his eyes off Pip. "Just you wait. You and Perci..."

"Will never happen. Just get that out of your

head. A guy will need a cage and a whip to tame that woman. She's a damned tiger."

"She saved our lives, too. I thought—" Matt forced himself to speak over the emotions threatening to choke him up. "That beam fell on the two of them, and I watched it happen. I couldn't do a damned thing to stop it. Pip was right beneath it, Nate. And then Perci jumped her. She knocked Pip out of the way; Perci had to know she'd be hurt doing it, possibly killed. And she just did it anyway. It landed on the both of them, and they were hurting, and I couldn't do a damned thing to help them. If it wasn't for Bowles...he helped me get them out. Perci just laid there, not making a sound. And it was burning on top of her. She didn't make a damned sound. Her arm was wrapped around her sister, and she was holding her. I'll never forget that." He stopped to fight a cough and take a drink of water his brother held out to him. "And Pip—Pip was trying to help Perci, and she couldn't. She was crying and trying to pull her sister free, more worried for Perci than herself. I thought they were both going to—Perci's going to be ok?"

Nate cleared his throat. "No lasting damage. Except a scar or two. Second-degree burn, at worst. She got lucky. It wasn't burning significantly at that point. It was just heavy. As for Pip... some burn scars, small ones. That'll be all she'll be able to see. It'll be the emotional scars that take the biggest toll. On them both. But she has her family to help her get through it. And ours. Am I to take it that there will be another Tyler sister living at our place soon?"

"As soon as I can get her to say yes." And in the meantime, Matt was just going to lie there and watch her sleep. But...

"Nate? I'm serious about those extension cords. You want me to stay hooked up to those damned machines, I'll need a much longer leash. I'm going to be next to her, no matter what."

74

Matt was holding her hand when Pip finally awoke.

She fought off the instinctive panic being in the hospital brought her and forced herself to stay calm. Matt was alive and looking down at her. Holding her.

Smiling.

Which meant...they were all ok, weren't they? "Matt, where's Perci?"

"Next door. I heard her yelling at Nate a few minutes ago. Well, trying to. Apparently, he threatened to chain her ass to the hospital bed if she so much as moved a muscle. And that's a direct quote."

His voice was hoarse beyond belief. His arm was in plaster, and he had stitches in his forehead. But he was alive and leaning over her—from a hospital bed that had been pushed up right next to hers.

"She's ok, honey. She did break her leg, and she'll have a scar where that damned rafter landed. But she'll be just fine eventually. We all three will."

"And Jay? What happened to him?" The last thing Pip remembered was Perci telling the EMTs —people her sister knew through the hospital— that Gunderson was an attempted murderer and her sister and Matt were to be treated first. The EMTs had listened.

It had been hard not to, with Jay Gunderson screaming over and over again that Matt needed to die, that Perci did, too, for trying to keep Pip away from him.

She'd never forget the things he'd been yelling or what he had tried to do.

Pip was not going to let herself be afraid of him anymore. He had almost taken everything from her this time. But she hadn't let him win. She had fought him herself. Fought for the people she loved most in the world.

And she had won.

It had been a team effort, but no one lived in a vacuum, did they? Family and loved ones and those she could trust—that was what mattered.

She loved the man looking down at her. Holding her, when he should have been lying down resting, healing. Taking care of himself instead of her.

If he was busy taking care of her all the time, who was taking care of him?

That was going to be her job from now on—showing him just how much she loved him. Trusted him.

Wanted him. Loved him. Was there any other way for her to put it, even to herself? She'd probably started trusting him the day he'd been there at the flooded river. Caring about him as the weeks had passed and they'd been together. Loving him the moment he'd given her Wind Lover, perhaps. Or the first time he'd ever kissed her.

Or the moment she'd realized he wanted her. That she mattered to him as much as he had grown to matter to her. Or when he had touched her for the first time in that barn.

It had only become clear to her when that

damned Jay Gunderson had almost taken him from her.

"I love you." It mattered that she be the first to say it, didn't it? That she be in control of this epic change in her future. It mattered.

He leaned down and kissed her lightly—she had a stitch or two in the side of her mouth where Gunderson had hit her—and whispered the words right back to her.

Pip reached out and wrapped one arm around him gently. He looked so banged up and battered, after all.

She just held him as close as she could.

Until his brother came in and forced Matt back into his own hospital bed. "Behave, you two. There will be plenty of time for that kind of stuff later. When you're both able to sing your ABCs at the top of your lungs again. And no making me an uncle before you're married. What would Mother say if you did that?"

Matt laughed. "Be good, Nate. Or I'll tell Mother all about the crush you have on Perci. And that you really need Mother's help to convince her of your feelings. How would you like that?"

"You are a horrible older brother, Matthew. But I am glad to see you're alive to torment me.

Now, back in your own bed. Or I'm ordering you moved across the room again."

"Just try it and see. I'm right where I belong. And this is where I am staying."

Pip was going to hold him to that. And she told him so as Nate finally stepped out of the room, leaving them completely alone.

They just stared at each other for a long, long time.

WHAT ABOUT PAN & LEVI?

There was a movie being made in Levi Masterson's front yard. And Levi's sweet, innocent, beautiful, wonderful, devilishly stubborn, twenty-two-year-old housekeeper was dressed in a skimpy fairy-witch costume. Parading around in front of at least three dozen people.

Distracting him from what he actually needed to be doing.

He didn't know what drove him more insane —the inconvenience of the movie crew or the woman he had wanted for months.

Levi watched as that damned film director Rowland Bowles, Hollywood's favorite hotshot, ordered everyone around in Levi's own front yard.

Including Levi's older brother Matt and sweet little sister-in-law.

Matt had been cast into the role of Clark's best friend, a struggling rancher trying to make ends meet at the property next to the more thriving one where Gretta—played by Pip—had grown up. Matt was Gretta's love interest.

Like Bowles would have ever been able to unwrap Matt and Pip long enough for another actor to take Matt's place.

They were using Pip's father's homestead as Matt's family ranch. Levi snorted at how that copied their real life. Pip was instrumental in running that ranch day to day, along with their father.

Everything was complicated and connected lately. Levi half felt he wasn't quite finding his way through.

Especially with her.

Almost from the moment he had met Pip's youngest sister, Pandora, he had known what he wanted. What was supposed to be, even. Levi was like that; when he knew what direction his life was going to take, he went after it full throttle. Until he had what he wanted. Needed.

Unfortunately, Pandora wasn't cooperating

No matter what Levi did, that girl just didn't seem to get the message that he was interested.

Levi was fast becoming the joke of their entire family.

Well, next to his brother Nate, anyway. Nate and Pip's identical twin sister, Perci, jointly held that title. The two of them fought and bickered constantly. Levi suspected it was because of the obvious and intense attraction between the two of them. They practically caught the room on fire the moment they entered. He wished he could say the same thing about him and Pan.

They could. If she would just stop being so damned stubborn.

It was too far-fetched, too crazy to even contemplate that their eldest brother, Joel, would fall for Phoebe Tyler. Shortly after, Matt went head over heels for Pip, Phoebe's younger sister. Nate and Perci seemed made for each other—and then there was Levi and Pandora.

Four brothers, four sisters. Crazy, far-fetched. Not really all that possible. But it had happened— or it would, if Pan ever caught on. And Nate stopped fighting Perci.

No wonder the entire town was talking.

It was no wonder some of his own friends had threatened to kick his ass for taking the last Tyler sister off the market—everyone just assumed Nate and Perci were inevitable.

Well, what was a man supposed to do? They lived in Masterson County, where attractive women—women in general—were outnumbered almost three to one. Pandora was the most gorgeous woman in the entire county. Gorgeous, sweet, loyal, brave, hardworking, beautiful, gorgeous, gorgeous, beautiful, wonderful. Perfect for him.

It might have been a mistake to tell his buddies to keep their paws off her at a county dance once, but how was he to know the woman would hold a grudge for more than six weeks? All through Pip's, Perci's, and Matt's recuperation after the barn had burned and they'd all been injured, after Pip and Matt's wedding, after all of that, you would think the woman would've forgiven him by now.

She still continued to question him about why he would do such a thing. She alternated between that and ignoring him—or treating him like a slightly stupid younger brother.

Dammit, Levi was tired of her looking at him like a brother. He was also tired of that idiot director Bowles putting his hands on her.

Something had to change, and soon. Before he went totally bonkers, gave his share of his ranch to his brothers, and moved to Australia to raise crocodiles or something. Or maybe head to Antarctica. Maybe that would put enough distance between him and the woman who invaded his dreams at night.

ALSO BY CALLE J. BROOKES

Falling

Hiding

Seeking

FINLEY CREEK SERIES

TRILOGY ONE (TEXAS STATE POLICE)

Her Best Friend's Keeper

Shelter from the Storm

The Price of Silence

TRILOGY TWO (FINLEY CREEK GENERAL)

If the Dark Wins

Wounds That Won't Heal

Hope for Finley Creek (bonus novella)

As the Night Ends

TRILOGY THREE (FINLEY CREEK DISASTER)

Before the Rain Breaks

Lost in the Wind

Walk Through the Fire

MASTERSON COUNTY NOVELLA SERIES

Seeking the Sheriff

Discovering the Doctor

Ruining the Rancher

Denying the Devil

SMALL-TOWN SHERIFFS

Holding the Truth

SUSPENSE/THRILLER

PAVAD: FBI CASE FILES

PAVAD: FBI Case Files #0001

"Knocked Out"

PAVAD: FBI Case Files #0002

"Knocked Down"

PAVAD: FBI Case Files #0003

"Knocked Around"

PAVAD: FBI Case Files #0004

"White Out"

PAVAD: FBI Case Files #0005

"Buried Secrets"

Calle has several free reads available at

www.**CalleJBrookesReads.com**

For my grandfather, the best man I have ever known.

You will be missed.

Oct. 2015

For my grandmother, who gave me the courage to try.
Without you and your love of romance, I never would
have made it this far.

Feb. 2016

For my papaw, whose children loved him deeply, and
will always miss him.

Oct. 2017

Calle J. Brookes enjoys crafting paranormal
romance and romantic suspense. She reads almost
every genre except horror. She spends most of her time
juggling family life and writing while reminding
herself that she can't spend all of her time in the worlds
found within books. CJ loves to be contacted by her
readers via email and at
www.**CalleJBrookes.com**. When not at home

writing stories of adventure and wrangling with two border collies and a beagle puppy, CJ is off in her RV somewhere exploring the beautiful world we live in, along with her husband of she can't remember how many years and their child.

www.ingramcontent.com/pod-product-compliance
Lightning Source LLC
Chambersburg PA
CBHW020345180626
46812CB00001B/352